Possible Worlds
and Other Stories

Possible Worlds
and Other Stories

Rachel Handley

• • •

ELLIPSIS IMPRINTS

2022

. . .

ELLIPSIS IMPRINTS
Durham, England

. . .

Twitter: @EllipsisImprint

Possible Worlds and Other Stories
Print edition ISBN: 978-1-8380723-7-7
Ebook edition ISBN: 978-1-0059898-2-8

"The Creature" first appeared in *365 Tomorrows*, January 2022 / "The Spaceship of Theseus" first appeared in *Full House Literary*, January 2022 / "The Sound" first appeared in *Sonder Magazine*, Runner Up, Panorama Flash Fiction Competition, April 2022 / "The Man of the Sand" first appeared in *Bear Creek Gazette*, Issue 9, May 2022 / "Judgement" first appeared in *Tree and Stone Magazine*, Queer as F* Issue, June 2022 / "Prime" first appeared in *Martian Magazine*, September 30, 2022

Cover design by Rachel Handley and Sara L. Uckelman.

For Nana

Contents

— 1 —

Possible Worlds

K EEPING track of the World-Doors was my duty for a century. It was one of the few lifer jobs left. Every Wednesday a new World-Door opened for a few seconds, spewed out some dust, then closed with a firm clap. My job was to monitor it. I would note how much dust escaped, and the time the World-Door closed. I'd never been told why anyone would pay for someone else to do this, but I didn't need to know why. A lifer job was one of the few jobs which guaranteed a cushy life. I always had enough food, and I could afford a home which was above the clouds of pollution that clung to each earth city. Anything was better than the mines. I refused to be a bent over old man covered in dirt all day long. Plus, there was no life guarantee if you worked in the mines. In this job I could live for as long as I liked and die when and how I wanted to.

On Wednesday a new World-Door opened, precisely on time. I waited for the dust it would usually sneeze all over the floor just before it shut. It typically took about two minutes for it to open and close, but instead it stayed open, funneling dust onto the floor like a split hourglass. I've been monitoring World-Doors for decades and not once has a door stayed open. We assumed that the dust must be a sign that the World-Doors had dead worlds on the other side of them. We imagined deserts devoid of life trickling sand into our world before they melted away.

The World-Door sat opaque in front of me. Its edges blurred and shifted in sharp waves as if it were uncomfortable. I wrote down its appearance, measured it with a tape measure. I even took a waist measurement and told it that it would look better in a suit than me. I'm ashamed to say it, but I started to get bored looking at it. Sure, it was an exciting thing in theory, but to me it was just an annoying sand-vomiting blob which had positioned itself directly in front of the kettle. I decided to poke it. As the tip of my middle finger slid into the middle of it, I was thrown to the floor. The World-Door pulsed and made a low-pitched humming sound.

"I wouldn't do that."

"Sorry. Sorr— I, wait. Are you talking to me?" I said.

"Who's 'you'?"

"I mean, well, you know, *you*." I advanced my finger towards it again and the door shot dust into my eyes. I screamed and the humming sound became louder.

"Sorry, OK, you don't like that." I kept blinking to get the sand out, tears streaming down my face. "You're, I mean, you're a door-thingy, a World-Door."

Silence.

"To other worlds."

Silence.

"Never mind. It's not important," I said.

"We agree. We have come to warn you."

I held up my hand. "OK, cool. But first, can you just slide over there? You've been in front of the kettle for a long time now."

"Sorry."

"Quite."

Weak electric shocks climbed up my spine as I put the kettle down. I turned to face the World-Door.

"Are you doing that?" I asked.

"What?"

"Electrocuting me. Are you electrocuting me?" I said.

"Only slightly." More sand.

"Only slightly!" I said.

"Yes. I'm glad you understand."

"I, bloody stop it," I said.

"We don't have time for this, Poking Being."

"My name is—"

"No time."

The World-Door started to pull me into it. My skin stretched as cold air curled around my limbs. I tried to step back, but stumbled under the pull. The World-Door grew to my height and width. I could not escape. A high pitch shriek rang in my ears. It was only later that I realised the noise was made by me. I grabbed the edges of the World-Door, but they collapsed under my fingers like wet sand. A new edge to the door was produced from within it, but it never held for long. The edge constantly remade itself. I was close enough now to see that the World-Door was not one large thing, but many. Each grain, each tiny particle, swirled around its guts like a tornado. Each small piece took its turn to form the shape of the door before it collapsed back into its centre. As my face slid into it, I heard a dull pop.

ಶಾ ಶಾ ಶಾ

My skin itched. I was face down on a scratchy sand-like substance. I looked up expecting to see something like a beach, but instead the ground looked entirely flat, smooth, and white. I realised that I could not trust my senses. The rough ground gnawed at my skin as I used my hands to stand up.

"What the—" I brushed the sand, or the dust, or whatever the hell it was off my trousers, ready to confront the World-Door, but it wasn't there. I turned around. No opaque blob, no electric shocks. I turned again, the sand shifting under my feet, yet all I could see was a continuous flat white surface.

"Hello?"

"Welcome." A World-Door emerged from beneath my feet. I stepped back quickly. As the World-Door rose the once smooth floor moulded itself into the oval shape of the door. Some grains of sand poured back onto my feet, others stuck to the emerging door and became a part of it. Each grain seemed to know where to go, like a microscopic puzzle reconstituting itself with perfect precision.

I stepped backwards. "Welcome to what exactly?" I said, trying to recover my cool.

"To the Multi-Doorway."

"Oh, well. That explains it then! And what exactly is that? And why the hell am I here?"

"It's the doorway to the worlds."

"I thought that was you! Are you not a door to worlds? Did you not wonder why I called you a World-Door?"

"No."

"Oh," I said. "Well, what are you?"

"Your help is required."

"What can I do? I just monitor World-Doors, or Doors? I don't know what to call you anymore."

"Unimportant." A few grains of sand fell to the floor. "Soon your world will die."

"What do you mean?" I asked.

"It will end its cycle."

"Yeah, I know what die means! I mean how, how will it die?" I wiped the sweat on my hands onto my trousers.

"If the possible worlds are not compressed, the universe will be stretched too thin."

The World-Door's edges rippled and puckered as bits of sand flaked off it. I suspected that it was trying to make itself resemble a human mouth. I don't know if it did this for my benefit, but I rather hoped not.

"Compressed?" I asked.

"The universe." The World-Door grew smaller, then bigger. *Was it thinking?* "The universe is much like your human skin. It can stretch, if it needs to, over a period of time, but if it is suddenly moved, it will break."

"Right? OK?" I asked.

"Growth is a feature of the universe, but if we let it grow without guidance it will split and whither. We must prune the excess to allow for it to flourish." "Prune the excess? You mean to kill off my world?" I looked at the World-Door for confirmation but received none. Its shape remained the same. My heartbeat rang in my ears.

"Kill off? No. Compress," it said.

"OK, but what is the difference?"

"We cannot kill your world, it is part of the universe. It cannot be destroyed. Compression is a mixing of worlds."

"Oh, so, you'd, er? You'd do the thing? Do er, OK, what would you do?" I asked.

"We will merge worlds and those worlds will grow together. Often the results are good for those worlds and their technology advances. Sometimes they are not an—"

"And you get some sort of war, right? All the sand?"

"The sand is often an outcome of the destruction of complex life."

"Right. So, this could kill my world after all?"

"Like many things it is possible, but not probable. We need someone to decide which worlds we should merge. We want to avoid some past mistakes by recruiting members of each world."

"I see. Mistakes?"

"It involved a very large moth." The World-Door grew smaller. "It was," the World-Door expanded, "not a very good outcome."

"OK, right. So, let's say I'm onboard, and I'm absolutely not saying this, how do I advise you?"

"You need to go to the worlds themselves."

"All of them?!"

"No, no, of course not. We have recruited enough people for the task, and many other beings from the other potential merge-worlds. You are not unique."

"Great. My own non-unique adventure."

The World-Door made no reply.

"So," I asked, "when do I start?"

"Now."

"No."

More sand dropped to the floor. "No?" said the World-Door, growing taller by a few feet. My feet sunk into the sand.

"I need to sort some stuff out before I start. I can't just pack up and leave my life, my job."

"We selected you because you can do just that." The door grew further.

"What?"

"You are alone."

I nodded. My job was not exactly a team effort. There were other people who monitored the World-Doors, but we've never met. There were no team meetings. No horrifying team building exercises. We knew what our main task was; observe and collect data about the World-Doors. Dedication to the job was the main thing they looked for in anyone wanting a lifer job. That, and the ability to be alone for most of the time. I'd never really liked what other people liked. I didn't care about going out with friends or eating good food. People irritated me, and given the choice, I'd pop a pill rather than ever eat again. I was a perfect candidate to be a lifer.

My job was glorified data entry, but at least it was a *lifer* job. If you worked in the mines, your life expectancy was around 40. If you worked above ground, you might make it to 60. The sickness ate away at people regardless of where they worked and lived, but it crept under the skin of the people who worked underground quicker than those above ground.

My people knew their history; they knew humanity used to live until 120. They knew the war had destroyed and robbed them of so much, including their precious last decades. Those decades were owed to them.

By the time they got the lifer tech right, I was an adult.

Businesses started to buy into the lifer companies, offering health benefits in the form of life extensions for their employees. But once the stories of trading power for lifer perks leaked anyone who had an extension was considered suspicious.

I started the job when I was 25 and hunting for something to do where I could both afford to live and avoid contact with other people. I'll never know when I would have died had I not taken the job, but I knew that I had, at 125, long gone past my normal life expectancy. The treatments which kept me alive required regular stays in a medical facility. They would knock me out and I'd wake up in pain. I usually recovered in three days, then went back to work. I never asked what they did, and they didn't tell me. Sometimes patients looked scared when they woke up. They always sat up too quickly and started to speak, but their words would come out as spit and gasping. A Meder—a doctor for lifers—soon shot them full of something soothing and lovely. I've never woken up scared. The time in the facility feels like a long sleep, one I am grateful for.

The government worried that the potential to extend your life far beyond a natural life span would lead to corruption, and it did. Though they only worried about this once many of them had sought life extension treatments. You might live to 150 with those treatments, maybe even 200, but immortal? No way. Still, the immorality myth, even though it is a myth, brought plenty of power with it. Big bosses whose job it was to sit on a mountain of money and hope the people crawling on the ground beneath them never looked up. Lifer jobs were naturally attached to well-paid jobs. Anyone from the majority class didn't have the same opportunities as people in any lifer sector. The world, already unbalanced, became even more so. Governments introduced new lifer jobs with increasingly vague role descriptions and politicians would trade their power on the promise of extended life. Years of trampling the majority took its toll on how the public perceived others. Some even thought people were either born worthy or unworthy of eternal life. But there were angry people in the majority too. People who didn't believe in born worth. They rose up and killed and slashed their way to a life they called fair and just. When I turned 50 lifer jobs were banned in all sectors but my own.

Lifer job recruitment was given a psychological overhaul to reduce the possibility of some megalomaniac becoming a lifer. Staff wanted, loners only. The suspicion of lifers grew into an easy hatred which fed into the culture. My sister wanted me to have a normal job, to be accepted by people. She knew

I didn't care about what strangers thought of me, so she took it upon herself to become my sense of social awareness whether I liked it or not. I did not, and I let her know it. The last time we spoke we screamed. I had taken a lifer job without telling her.

I mentioned my new job over breakfast—her: muesli, fruit juice, banana; me: black coffee. She threw my coffee at me, and I walked out. I didn't even pack my things, I just went straight to the head office, told them I needed to start earlier than planned and they said OK. My training began then. Most of it was not on the job itself, monitoring when a World-Door appears is simply a means of paying attention. Paying attention when something new happens is not hard. Paying attention when everything is the same is the worst thing in the world. Your eyes ache, you overthink old memories, and start to sing to yourself. The training weans you off that kind of response to nothing happening. It trains you to deal with boredom as if you were witnessing a thousand exciting things.

My sister must have died many years ago, but to me she is still 22, screaming at me for taking the job while hot coffee drips from my nose onto my shirt. I thought of her when the World-Door asked me to help it. I wanted to tell her: See, see, being a lifer isn't just eternal nothing, or corruption, it has a purpose! Look at this cool thing I'm doing.

"I still want to go back. I want to say goodbye."

The World-Door rippled and moved to the floor to suck more sand into its membrane.

"To who?"

"To the world."

"One hour is permitted."

The World-Door reassured me that it would spit me out at the same time and place that it had pulled me in. I slid across the floor leaving a trail of sand. I looked around the room expecting some sort of change, like a physical announcement of the difference between yesterday and tomorrow. I found my mind returning to the mundane things I'd miss; the fat grey couch which tried to absorb you when you sat down, my favourite mug which was ugly but huge.

Despite there being only a ladder between my work area and my bed I still fell asleep in the armchair I installed right in front of where the World-Door appeared. It was a perfect observation spot. I'd sit in it and pretend I was the old man I really was. Though I didn't look more than 30, I could feel the years in my bones, in my energy to keep doing things. I used to relish going to my quarters, now I spend almost all my hours in the same place. Being pulled through the door felt like a slap, you can't be an old man when you're a lifer, only eternally the same.

The World-Door deposited me in my quarters. I cleaned the sand off and I swept it into the bin. I sent a note to my boss, Mr. Oak. Not her real name, of course, but the company liked distance between colleagues. No one wanted a loner to become gregarious after a few decades. I added today's data and a few extra comments about the World-Door and its apparent sentience. I did not tell Mr. Oak everything, but I sent a good enough overview. The main thing I wanted to know was whether the company already knew the World-Doors were sentient, and if traveling with one was dangerous. For all I knew the company wanted us to make contact like this and expected it to happen eventually, but that seemed unlikely. Surely, they would train us for something so important if they thought it would happen.

"Do I proceed?"

No answer. An hour had passed. I sat in the armchair, waiting. I heard it before I saw it, an electric whip struck me across the face first, then the arms. Sand from the bin poured out and travelled up my legs to my head covering my eyes. I heard the World-Door's gaping mouth crackle with light. The sand itched my face. As the World-Door folded its mouth over my head I saw my work screen light up. A message just out of reach.

No. Dangerous. Report to HQ.

ða ða ða

Training with the World-Doors was focused on the physical. My main concern was how to stop vomiting whenever I travelled too quickly between worlds. Excessive portal travel does a number on your innards.

I trained with one other person: Anna. She had been a World-Door monitor for longer than me, but she wouldn't give me an exact number. Whenever I tried to talk to her about anything outside of our mission, she interrupted me to tell me about different, and, according to her, excellent, leaves. She'd list off her favourite ones whilst staring at the sand on the floor.

"I dunno, leaves are nice, I guess," I said.

"Just nice? Have you seen a Victoria Amazonica? They are water lilies the size of a man and very excellent."

"I'm just going to believe you on this one," I said. Anna muttered something under her breath.

"Let's just get back to training, OK?"

I nodded.

Anna skipped a few pages in her notebook. A non-electronic writing device made from material which could withstand traveling through multiple World-Doors. Everyone had a similar notepad and were instructed to use it for their reports. No screens, no computers, nothing electronic.

"All mission objectives are the same; locate any doubles of yourself, place a tracker on them, report back."

"Oh, well that's easy. I was expecting something more complex."

"Trust me, it's not easy. Seeing your double is very disorienting and placing the tracker on them is extremely dangerous."

"Dangerous? Why do you need to track them?"

Anna looked at the sand between her feet. "Tracking keeps you safe. Now, let's just try to get you to stop throwing up." She was still looking at the sand. "You'll be fine as long as you practise and take the serum before you go to a new world," said Anna.

Anna was in charge of a few other people and would instruct me to practise stepping in and out of the World-Door while she trained them. Whenever I asked about communicating with HQ the World-Doors would dismiss the suggestion. I asked around the other trainees and they seemed curious but not worried. None of them had had any word from HQ about the World-Doors and as far as I could tell their arrival to the multi-doorway was much like my own; sudden and unexpected. I needed to find out more, but this was not the right place to search for answers. The World-Doors said nothing of use whenever I questioned them. They were deliberately obtuse, as was Anna. I needed to get back to my monitoring station, talk to Mr. Oak, and figure out what the hell was going on. For the company to not warn us about World-Door's sentience meant they probably had no idea about it, or they did, and they decided not to tell the people who would be most likely to interact with them. Either way, there was something off.

Time moved differently in the multi-doorway. The reason why the World-Doors could send me back to the exact time and place I left my office was because World-Doors essentially poked a hole in space-time for a particular world and funneled what they liked into it. If you pushed something into a world, something had to come back out. Usually it was dust, or sand, sometimes liquid. Anna told me a large batch of squirrels once emerged during an exchange, but I think she was taking the piss.

I travelled to my first possible world at night. It was raining and I had landed in a large puddle. I got up, trousers soaking wet, and looked around. I had been expecting something more surreal, but I felt like I was standing on the street I used to live on. I could see this world's version of my house. I knew that I'd travel to a similar world, of course, but I didn't realise it would be this similar.

I figured that going to see my own house to see if a version of myself lived there would be a good way to begin. If I didn't exist in this world, then I could start my investigation by exploring my own timeline. I walked up to my house slowly, trying not to look out of the ordinary. I didn't want my neighbours to think I was an inexplicably soggy burglar. The kitchen and porch light were both on. Seeing the small sturdy house with its familiar red bricks made me feel like I was watching my life from a TV set; I was there but only at a distance. I got to the edge of the window and dipped my head under the frame so I wouldn't be spotted.

As I did so I fell hard onto the ground. Something had crashed into me.

"Fool," she said.

"Anna?!"

She narrowed her eyes.

"What are you doing here? Didn't you go to another possible world?"

"I followed you." She shrugged. "I'm here in yours to stop you doing something horrendous."

"What do you mean? Do—did—er—do I mess up?" I heard a familiar tune and turned my head to the right to listen. I always whistled when I washed the dishes, now I could hear someone else doing the same.

"The guy whistling?"

"Is you, yes," Anna said.

"And that's bad?"

"How do you think the World-Doors merge worlds, Alex?"

"I, the tracker? Er—"

"They use us to bust worlds open. They merge them together with chaos."

"How do you know?"

"Because I've seen it."

"So if I say hi to past Alex, I'll die?"

"No."

"Oh?"

"We'll all explode."

"Well, that's much worse."

"Plus you'll die." Anna looked at me and frowned.

"What do we do?"

"We need to avoid the chaos, even you being here in a world that doesn't belong to you, is starting to draw your world and this one together. What the World-Doors have engineered are not quick blink of the eye compressions. You don't just observe your other self, track them, and report back for the World-Doors to take over. Our visiting the worlds is what starts the process of compression. Compression of worlds is a global natural disaster, like one planet trying to break open another by crashing into it. We need to destroy the World-Doors," said Anna.

"I'm confused. Didn't you say we'd explode if I said hi to other-me?"

Anna looked at me and frowned. "I did."

"But compression of worlds is a slow natural disaster?"

She sighed. "Yes, it is. You saying hi to your other self would speed the compression up, and be bad for you personally, but it's also bad for the world. Your simply being here starts the whole process. The point is, you're a catalyst. We all are."

"How do we destroy them?"

Anna grabbed my arm and pulled me away from the house.

"I don't know," she said.

"Oh." I waited for her to say something else, but she stared at me instead. "Please blink," I said.

"Yes, sorry." She itched her eyes. "I forgot."

"I know," I said. "So." I moved my arm away from her and she let go. "You don't know how to destroy them?"

"No" she said. "The only thing I can think of is to induce a paradox while they make a visitation to a possible world, to catch them in the compression itself. But it's risky, and we might die, and I'm not prepared to save the world if it means I'll die."

"I get it," I said. She stared at me again.

"Er?" she gestured to me.

"I mean, me too. I'm strictly a no death in exchange for the world person."

Anna nodded. "We need more people, all of the recruits. I've been piggy-backing onto other's world visitations or using training to get the word out. Not everyone is as convinced as I am, but there might be enough of us now to do something to stop the World-Doors."

Anna walked in front of me. I occasionally checked I hadn't gone in the wrong direction, but I spent most of the walk watching her handprint on my arm fade. It had an outline like snail slime, but nicer, more like very fine glitter mixed up with glue. I tried to wipe it off, but I couldn't.

"Damn it!" I had stepped in the puddle again. We'd walked to our original entry point for Possible World #78. I saw the puddle shimmer, then return to normal. I shook my head, then my foot. A hallucination?

Anna tapped the device on my wrist; it looked like a shabby watch. If you ping it, a World-Door answers and takes you to your next assigned world. She was going to piggyback on my journey again. If anyone asked, I had requested in-field training from her because of an emergency.

I shook my foot again. The water from the puddle had grown up my trouser leg, "Heraclitus would be happy," I said. Anna looked at my leg, then my grin, and said nothing.

A World-Door opened next to Anna. Its mouth opened, the edges of it bent the ground underneath with such force that the ground started to buckle underneath it. Anna stepped through. The mouth shrank, puckered with a dull pop, then expanded.

I walked towards the door slowly. Normally, I'd throw myself in, but I noticed the water on my shoe and trousers glimmer, as if oil had been mixed in with it. Every few seconds I felt compelled to stare at it. And each time I looked down the line of damp on my trousers had risen. I decided to ask the World-Door if they knew whether there was something odd about the water in this world. As I put my foot forward two hands grabbed my shoulders and pulled against the force of the World-Door.

"Absolutely not," a voice said.

I stumbled backward. The top of my shoe had been cut off. The tips of my toes had been cut through; the top of my shoe and foot had, seemingly, left with Anna through the World-Door. There was no pain, no blood. The glittering substance from the puddle sat on the edges of my shoe like a balm. It was as if the tips of my toes had never existed. I reached down to touch the top of my big toe; it now resembled a very neat square. I felt my hand touch it, and I felt my foot being touched, but neither sensation felt real. It felt like a memory.

"Some lifer you are," the man said.

"Some lifer?" I replied, twisting up from my feet to face him. "I am very much a lifer, thank you."

The man raised both eyebrows at me and shook his head. I waited for him to reply. Nothing. He stared at me.

"Your shoe?" he said.

"Yes," I said, looking at his face for the first time since the man's arrival. The man had long white hair and a long white beard. He reminded me of a fantasy novel wizard, and if it weren't for his sleek black suit, I would have thought he was at least a little bit magical.

"Does it hurt?" he asked.

I looked down to my foot again. "No. Oddly, not at all."

"Good" he said, "that means we still have time."

"Ti—" I began.

"Can you walk on it?"

"Walk on it?"

"Your foot. People usually use them to walk," he said.

"Oh. Yes. Yes, I can. I think." I walked around as if I was trying on new shoes that were slightly too big. I could walk.

"Good," he said. "Follow me." He turned and started walking in front of me.

"Er. Hold on. Who are you? You think I'll just start following you?"

The man turned to face me. "It's clear that the World-Doors are perhaps not too friendly, isn't it? They chopped off," the man sighed "Do you think you'd be alive if you'd gone all the way through?"

"No." I paused, realising. "Anna" I said.

"Who cares about her. We need to go."

"That's awful. She was a friend, sort of. She was alive! That matters!"

The old man cast his eyes down. "She is alive, in a sense."

"So, she's alive? But then, what? Who is she? And who the hell are you?" I said.

"Anna is no longer the Anna you've known. I suspect the last jump she made through the World-Door clinched it.

"I don't understand. What is happening?"

"She's a World-Door."

"She's. A. World. Door?"

"Good god, it's like you know nothing. What kind of a lifer are you? We are the guards of the World-Doors! Did you think you were just looking at a portal all day for nothing? You were monitoring it, containing it in its place!

You were meant to stay clear from it. You were certainly not meant to go in. I've never heard of anyone so—"

"OK, I get it. I suck at my job."

"I would use much stronger language than that."

"When it sucked me in and showed me its world, it answered all of my questions. I felt like I finally understood my job, that I was meant to help them!"

"Nonsense. You failed to use any sense! Did you not ponder their words?" The old man's voice was getting louder as he spoke. I stood back from him, inch by inch.

"I—"

The old man sighed and gained some composure. He stood up straighter as a car pulled up. I started to move away but he nodded at me, signaling to me that he had expected the arrival of a car.

"So, who are they? The World-Doors I mean?"

"Prisoners," he said.

"And what am I?" I asked.

"That is yet to be determined."

The car door opened from the inside.

🙚 🙚 🙚

The man's hand slapped the outside of the car window, shutting the door with such force that I felt a breeze. I looked forward, no lights, no sound. Just the faint outline of a man in the driver's seat and my breath. The cold air clung to my skin, I felt inspected by it. The man got in at the front and asked the driver to go. I heard the doors next to me lock. The car started and we drove at a steady space through what looked like the same street each time; rows and rows of the same house, with only numbers to tell them apart.

The man said nothing, and I didn't know what to say, so I looked forward and put my hands on my knees. The pressure of the silence sat in my throat. I knew I needed to speak first.

"They're prisoners?"

"Yes," said the man. He was looking forward. I wondered if he was consciously trying not to look at me too. The glitter around my foot and leg was moving up towards my torso. It illuminated my feet.

"Why?"

"What?" he said.

"Why are they prisoners?"

"Because they hate our way of worlds."

"You mean way of life?" I asked.

"No. I made no mistake. They hate our way of worlds."

"Wha—"

He waved a hand in my direction. "A way of worlds is how a world operates, its physical laws."

"They hate, wait, let me get this right. They hate physics?"

"Not quite. They hate laws."

"Er—"

The man sighed and looked me in the eye. "They hate anything with regularity and mean to destroy it."

"So, they hate that our world has laws which govern how things work?"

"Yes."

"But how do you even destroy something like a law?" I asked.

"By merging worlds. You merge enough of them, and the newly formed world becomes a heap of random junk. Laws fire off against one another until you get chaos. I assume your friend, Anna, is from one of these chaos worlds. We can, as you must understand, not permit the World-Doors to succeed. Life in a world without any regularity would be—"

"Shitty," I said.

"Well, yes. That certainly is one way to put it," he said.

"But why would they try to kill me?"

"Because your life is one of the anchors of this world. Killing you peels a layer of regularity from the world. Kill enough anchors and you can merge a world; merge a world and you get chaos."

"But why bother? I just don't get why they would want to go to this much effort to destroy things—people!" I said.

The man closed his eyes slowly. Another sigh.

"Their aim is to survive, but they do it at the cost of everything else. So, we imprisoned them as best we could. Linking them with regular timers so they appear every Wednesday in labs around the regular worlds. Noting their appearance. Keeping them in place. But it seems they have gained control of these devices and we cannot contain many of them anymore."

"So what will you do? How do we stop them?" The car pulled up to an office building.

"We need to capture them," he said.

"How?"

He got out of the car, walked around it, then opened my door. "That's where you come in."

He walked slightly ahead of me towards a run-down warehouse, his pace was quick, and I had to consciously move quicker to keep up.

"Sorry, I what? Need to capture them? And where are we going?" I asked, as if the warehouse wasn't the only building on the street.

"Yes," said the man. He did not turn to look at me.

"All of them?"

"Yes."

"How?"

The warehouse looked like it had been constructed from thick plates of iron. The old man turned to look at me, and for the first time, he smiled. The corners of his mouth lifted up his beard.

"You'll be bait," he said, still smiling.

He pressed his thumb onto the wall of the building and an outline of a door appeared. It was made of the same thick metal as the walls. The man strained as he opened it. He gestured that I should enter first, but I stayed where I was, I could not see inside, there was no light.

"Bait?" I said. The man held the door open with great effort; cold recycled air washed over me.

"Yes. You're an anchor in several worlds, each version of you keeps the timelines from your respective worlds glued together. If they locate each version of you from their worlds and destroy them, they'll be able to merge a catastrophic number of possible worlds. I don't think they can resist such an opportunity, do you?"

"I don't know, I guess?"

The man nodded as if I'd agreed to help.

"Great!" He put his hand on the middle of my back and pushed but I tensed my legs and held the side of the door to stay in my place.

"You pushed me!" I said.

"You weren't going in!" The man said.

"Right. Exactly. I still don't know why I'm so important. But all that aside, it's weird that you are trying to shove me into a dark room."

"Oh," he said, "the lights are automatic." The man waved his hand past the doorway and a row of lights along the corridor lit up revealing the inside of the building to be just as grey and dull as the exterior of the building.

"Oh," I said. "And why am I im—"

"Mr. Oak."

"My boss?" I said. The memory of my sending a message to her sloshed around my head.

"Yes," said the man. "My boss too. Without her we wouldn't have any of this." He gestured to me again that I should go inside, and I followed.

"We've never met. Is that weird? To have never met your boss?" I said. I tried to use the click of our footsteps on the metal floor to regulate my heartbeat.

The man did not reply.

"I guess not," I said.

The man ignored me and looked at the large black door at the end of the corridor instead.

"Get ready for a reunion," he said.

"A reunion? I just said we've never met."

The man opened the door at the end of the corridor. Natural light. I stepped onto grass.

"What the—"

I was standing in a garden. A glass dome ceiling let in natural light, there were flowers, and birds. Insects approached me for a quick inspection, then quickly became bored.

"The ceiling is glass? I got the impression you wanted to be a secret organisation! One helicopter on a stray ride and you're discovered."

The old man gestured to the people sitting on the grass to be quiet. He sat on the bench to the left of us. A small stream hurried past his feet and mine, then disappeared into the earth.

"I think Mr. Oak should be the one to explain," said the old man.

"Hi, Alex" said Mr. Oak.

"What, what, what, what—"

"Normally you'd say hi back."

"What! No! Yes. Yes. Normally I'd said hi back, normally I'd be normal, but I've just found out my boss is my sister, so please permit me to be less than fucking normal."

"You were never quite normal," she said.

"Martha."

"Mr. Oak," she said.

"Mr. Oak, hello," I said.

Martha nodded. "Now, let's begin. This warehouse is a safe house. It is a place where duplicates can escape from being killed by the World-Doors."

"Pretty snazzy safe house."

"Yes, well, we've had thousands of years to generate capital."

"Thousands?"

"Yes. We have been operating for longer than you think."

'But the technology was only invented a few hundred years ago," I said.

"Yes. It was."

"So?"

"So! What does that suggest to you?"

"That you're annoying."

"Alex. Think about it. The duplicate you saw in this world. He was in his old house, yes? He was younger than you, yes? He wasn't a lifer yet?"

"I didn't get a proper look at him, but I guess he was like a younger version of me. I just figured he'd already had life enhancement in this world."

"He hasn't. The duplicate is a younger version of yourself."

"So, World-Door travel is traveling through time?"

"Not exactly," said Mr. Oak, "traveling to different times is possible, of course, but you're always traveling to a different possible world when you do so. Worlds need a time point for any kind of connection to hold long enough for you to jump through."

"Let me guess, the time point is linked to the anchor somehow?"

"Yes."

I sat on the grass under my feet. Everyone except for Martha and the old man had left the room. I saw another stream of water emerge, then disappear. Nothing here felt real.

"OK, so I'm an anchor, but so what? So are loads of people. Why can't someone else help you out, why can't you do it?"

"I can't jump different worlds; I can only send messages between them. I'm Mr. Oak in most of the worlds we've connected to."

"How?"

"Well, we have Word-Doors of our own."

"You mean, you captured one?"

"Yes. Though they do not live long." Martha nodded to the old man. "Lead the way, Mr. Ash."

"What will you do when you run out of tree names?"

Martha slapped my arm. "Shut up, Alex."

❧   ❧   ❧

I spent the next few days in the warehouse. The other areas of the warehouse were more of what I had expected, boring grey, far too much metal. There were quarters for everyone, so there was some privacy at last. I couldn't get Martha to say anything about her life to me though. She avoided me and sent lackeys in her stead when she needed information from me or wanted me to see something. They let me see the captured World-Door on day three. I expected horrors and to never sleep again, but the room it was kept in was quite nice. The enclosure was round with a corridor circling around it. You could see inside pretty well, but not at every angle. There were metal walls constructed in places, giving the space a sense of privacy. What surprised me was the furniture, a couch, a bookcase with books, a gramophone. It felt so human. There was a kitchen area, even a TV. I stood and watched the World-Door, sand slowly spilt onto the floor as its edges moved very slightly. It was very small. The smallest I'd encountered so far.

I pressed my hand on the glass to see if it would do anything, but it just poured more sand out, then ate it again. I took my hand off the glass, leaving a print of my fingers which I tried to rub off with my jumper. I didn't see the old man, Mr. Ash, approach. He seemed to walk silently, as if he existed above the ground at all times.

"Nice, isn't it? Nicer than my accommodation anyway." He was fiddling with the end of his beard.

"Mine too," I said.

The old man inhaled as if he was going to speak but said nothing.

"Why?" I said.

"Why what?" The old man was twisting the end of his beard with both hands now.

"Why does the World-Door have nicer quarters than us both?"

"Well, because she deserves it after all this time, don't you think?"

"She? What?"

"My god. Mr. Oak didn't debrief you?"

"She's not speaking to me, it seems."

"The World-Doors are created, not born," said the old man.

"What?" said Alex.

"They were human," said the old man. He stroked his beard. "Well, most of them were."

"Fuck off! What? Most of them were human?" said Alex. The old man stopped stroking his beard and frowned.

"Sorry, I'm just shocked. I figured they were some kind of alien species," said Alex.

"Well, some of them used to be, but that's not the point. The point is that the World-Doors used to be anchors of their possible worlds."

"Honestly, I just don't believe you," said Alex. The old man raised his eyebrows.

"It doesn't matter if you don't believe me. You're stuck here anyway," said the old man.

"Stuck? You can't trap me."

"You're already trapped. We are all. Each one of us in an anchor, so we must be kept hidden from the World-Doors."

"I'm one of them?" I looked at the World-Door, its dull light danced over the sand on the floor.

"Alex," said Martha. She had walked up to me in perfect silence. I jumped.

My sister didn't look real to me. I had mourned her death decades ago, alone. Resigned to her natural death and my extended one. Now that she was here, I felt I couldn't trust what I saw in front of me.

"Alex," she said again.

"I'm one of them?" I pointed to the World-Door. It had moved closer to the glass between us.

"Technically, no and yes."

I look from Martha to the old man. "Well, that's helpful. Thanks so much. Please just tell me what the hell is going on."

"I am doing, look, anchors have the ability to jump words naturally, usually they lose this ability in childhood. So, you don't see kids randomly popping up then disappearing. But not everyone loses the ability, and some can be retrained for it. The World-Doors are a result of attempted retraining by our government. People pushed to their limit trying to move back and forth between worlds. It tore them apart."

"Why though? I know governments don't tend to be awesome, but needlessly putting people through pain. Why?"

"You are less cynical than me." She held up her hand to stop my reply. "Possible worlds are lucrative. Imagine having access to worlds where oil hasn't been taken from the land, or where gold is seen as useless metal? Being able to access those worlds and resources could provide governments with enormous wealth and power."

"So, they tortured people for profit?"

"Essentially, yes."

"But you've captured one?"

"To revert them to their human state. We think we have a way to do it."

"And in the meantime, we are all trapped here?"

"Yes, well, not trapped per se, you can leave if you want to, but it would be dangerous. We've made this building to not allow unregistered World-Doors to enter. If they could, they would have swarmed this place by now and made you into one of them."

"Jesus."

"Yeah."

"Well, I guess I'll go have a nice sit down then. Have a holiday, relax."

"Not quite," said Martha. "I'm still your boss, and you're still a lifer with a mission."

"I thought as much, go on, what is it."

"You're going to travel to possible worlds under supervision to bring back other anchors here, just like Mr. Ash did for you."

"How exactly?"

"Well, via your friend Anna. We figu—"

"Anna?" I looked into the enclosure. "Anna." I pointed at the World-Door.

Martha cleared her throat. "We figured you'd be able to get through to her. We need her to move you safely to different worlds, once we've collected enough anchors, we can start them on medicine to prevent them being turned into World-Doors. Eventually, we want to cure everyone. We want to help them, and it begins with you."

I put my hand on the glass. "Hi, Anna."

— 2 —

The Creature

O K, NOW, before you see it, just—"

"Just what, Terry?"

"Just stay calm, be calm, I mean."

Terry opened the door and pointed at a pink creature on the lamppost.

"There's nothing there, where is it?"

"Look up," Terry said, jabbing his finger in the exact same direction as if that was helpful.

Adam moved closer to Terry's arm. "I see it. You absolute bell-end, how did it even escape?"

"Well, the specimen seemed inert, so I just popped to the kitchen for a coffee."

"For a coffee." Adam was expressionless.

"For a coffee. And before I knew it the bloody thing was crawling up a lamppost."

"Well. What did you get me here for? Just capture it!"

"That might be a bit tricky," said Terry.

"Why?"

"Because, well, um, it's eaten already."

"You let it eat. You let it eat?"

"I didn't let it do a fucking thing, it scampered past me like a shitty little rat, OK?"

"OK."

"So, it's eaten a few lampposts already."

Adam looked at the specimen. Its pink gelatinous body, now bloated and round, was starting to curl around the lamppost and nibble the top of it.

"We are fucked," said Terry.

"No," said Adam. "You're fucked, I'm off for a pint."

"It'll eat your pint!"

22

Adam walked off; the single finger raised on his hand singled his goodbye.

Exhibit 1: Transcription of Dr. Sarah Hall's last Daily Log on the experiment
I first met the creature in my dreams. The small pink blob seemed innocent enough. I'd push it into different shapes, bounce it like a ball, and wish it was real when I woke up. My obsession with dreams grew as I got older, I read everything about them, the tat as well as the scientific. I tried to control my dream-self, tried to figure out how my brain could contain such wonder. My profession was fated by my obsession: Could I bring a dream to life? The scientific community laughed at me, of course, but I pursued my experiments in the lab after work hours. When I succeeded, after years, to extract something from a dream and make it real I was surprised that the small pink blob, my friend during my childhood, was the thing which sprung to life. Though I'd investigated dreams for years, I'd not thought, or dreamed, about the pink blob since I was about seven. Still, better than nothing I thought. I'd make the news with this! And I did. The moment it arrived the creature set about eating my desk. It had no obvious mouth but seemed to simply ingest whatever it landed on. I told it to stop, but it didn't seem to understand me. The desk gone, it started on the broken computer on the floor. Then the floor itself. I tried to grab it, but it oozed through my hands tearing pieces of my skin as a warning. It tore through the floor, down six of them if I counted correctly. Burst pipes and water trailed behind it. "Stop! Where are you going?" I shouted, as if speaking to a naughty pet. Then a shriek from below. I looked down the hole it had made. The blob was slithering back to me. The leaking water and falling debris caused it no concern. It flung itself at great speed onto me.

"Mother," it said, as its body ripped into my skin.

Exhibit 2: Newspaper Clipping from Circa 2043
Dear 12499,
We blobs have a saying: blob not to blob, but only to blob blob. But this saying, this terrible warning about love—that we blobs should not love, only feed—is nonsense. Oh, my love, my dearest 12499. Don't you realise, we need only each other to live. (That and a planet to consume, but with my blob wealth we will be most content). How sweet are your pink curves, how luscious your transparency! Oh 12499, please, please will you reconsider? Will you make me the happiest blob on planet 33990000 and consume the wicked earth with me?

Truly yours, 56883

The Spaceship of Theseus

IT IS common, with my kind, to live for centuries. But those centuries are not without cost. When I finally returned to the land I wondered if I would snap. My skin's taut mass begged for space, for relief from the thick air of the earth. I remember when we first approached Athens. We moved in formation with the security sky-ships to ensure we landed well and without interference. Compact spaceships, new and rich with life, descended towards the land in front of me. I lumbered behind them, creaking. Home. Triumphant. The humans swelled with pride and rubbed their limbs at the thought of escape from the recycled air and food pouches. Captain Theseus had won his battle by persuasion. I had won by staying alive. Honour, he told me patting my side, would be shared by us all.

Once we docked in Athens, the humans left me. Their faces were lined with deep creases and wide smiles, they looked like they belonged on the ground. I felt like a hollow bone. No longer of practical use, I became a symbol: Theseus's ship. My captain would come to see me each day, pat my shoulder, and leave in silence. He reassured me I would fly again. I longed to feel like the only thing alive for miles. I wanted my journeys to be measured in years.

I started to rot. The earth air ate at the seams of my body. Most ships are recycled once they land, but they kept me as I was. I told them the rot was death. If I was unable to move my mind to a new ship, I would be their prisoner. They laughed as if I had made a joke. They replaced me inch by inch until they agreed to move my mind. A new body, finally. But this was not my fate. I was placed in a glass box and put on exhibition next to the replaced parts of my body. The ship, though each part had been replaced, retained the name "Theseus' Ship." I sat next to it with no label. When people walked past, I would ask "what am I?" and they would pause, frown, and never look at me again.

Twin Earth

EVERYONE gets there in different ways. Some people only have to think about it, no effort at all, and they appear in the main exchange centre. Others, like me, who aren't blessed with the ability, have to pay to board one of the transfer trains. The fare is paid in memories, the juicier the better. There is only one exchange centre in the city. Its walls are of rough stone, the only place in the city that didn't look like it's frosted glass. The inside is coated in strips of steel. Granite sits between each strip like a gangly tree root. The payment machines sit in a row by the entrance. You can't go anywhere you like in the city. Well, you can if you think yourself there, but if you're like the rest of us, you'll need a ticket. Even then, a ticket for entry only gets me to Tearth, I'm barred from most buildings. Those who can will themselves to where they want to be are not so confined. We can still go to bars, but bars get tiring fast when it's the only thing you can do. You may as well not travel at all.

Tearth didn't start out like this. When it was first discovered it was seen as a land of new adventure and discoveries. It was also, conveniently, a land the scientists could finally point to and claim they weren't crazy for believing in. They'd been ridiculed in the scientific community for years for studying extra sensory travel, yet somehow retained partial government funding despite media onslaught from the get-go.

The ride to Tearth was usually pretty full. Lots of people on here were posh and wanted you to know about it. You know the type, multi-platform shoes, not skinny one-platforms like me. If they were feeling extravagant, a hat. All genders love a good, obnoxious, hat. Most people get the kind with virtual birds which fly and dip around their owner. The posh folk looked annoyed when I walked into the compartment, like they couldn't believe they had to take the exchange with the likes of me. I wanted to sit closer to them and get dirt on them. *Whoops, sorry, clumsy old worker being clumsy!* I'd say, coughing and spluttering on their faces. I'm not actually dirty. But fear, when it is great enough, can craft its own reality.

When I first heard of Tearth I thought it was a joke, most people did. Now here I am on my way to the main T-Lab. I got a message from them a few days ago. Very official.

> Dear Mr. Dor,
>
> We invite you to participate in our Tearth trial. We will compensate you 600 treeks and restore all memories ever submitted to the exchange. To agree, please press the screen with your thumb. To disagree, please say no to the screen after the beep. If you accept, the address to our T-Lab will be encoded into a new memory which you can access during your travel to us.
>
> We look forward to welcoming you.
>
> Signed,
>
> M.

The letter came on the day I lost my job. It was not a job I loved, just a typical rebuild job to patch up the city, but I needed to eat. Most people were dedicated to the rebuild. It felt useless to me. The ground shook so much sometimes that entire buildings fell in one slump to the floor, undoing everyone's work from the past month. The tremor alarms would go off before anyone got hurt, but the mess of it was terrible. Entire homes crushed in seconds. Before the alarms were created, families were extinguished too. But the corporations realised how many hands were needed to rebuild the world brick by brick, so they installed alarms. If they ever found a way to not use us, we would find ourselves under a pile of rubble soon enough. 600 treeks is not to be sniffed at. I planned to find a rebuilding job once I came back from Tearth. They are easy enough to find, as easy as they are to find as they are to lose. I packed up my porta-home, strapped it to my bag, and left.

The posh woman next to me had moved so close to the edge of her seat that she was almost falling off. I coughed at her and a little bit of spit rolled down her cheek. She made a high-pitched sound, said something in First Earth, then moved to a different compartment. I put my porta-home bag on her seat just before another posh lad approached it. He asked me to move it, speaking purposefully slow. Normally I'd show him what I thought of him, but 600 treeks, I wasn't going to get thrown back to Earth. No. I quietly moved my bag. The posh lad moved as far away from me as the lady had.

We are now approaching TEARTH. Please place the mask over your face before resting your arm on the injector pad.

The announcement sounded like it was made by a hollow robot, one of those old sentient synths which used to run everything; transport, cooking, anything which used to have electric in the ancient world, ran on minds in the new. They used to be everywhere.

I put my arm on the pad. A strap wrapped itself around my arm, and a sharp pain spread from my hand to my shoulder. Everyone knew about the injections, some people welcomed them because it was the only thing which made it possible for normal people to travel to Tearth.

When I was first injected, I knew what was going to happen, they warn you several times before you board and make you sign a consent form. But a form can't really prepare you for what it was like. The injection puts your body into a kind of semi-conscious stasis. It's like moving in and out of a dream where you know you're dreaming yet can't quite get back to reality. It's not even nice and imaginative, you just see a distorted version of the compartment you're in. And though you feel like you are in control, you aren't really. You can't remove the strap mid-journey, though I've tried a few times.

They knew, once we got to the Tearth port, that I'd tried to remove the strap. I got a warning, and they suggested I wouldn't be able to travel next time if I did it again. Obviously, I tried it again. Four times, actually. Each time, a warning. Each time, no ban. So I figured two things. They were watching me, and they wanted me to keep taking journeys to Tearth. I stopped going after realising this. I didn't like being their little toy. But the letter, oh boy that letter. That made me change my mind. Money, yes please, a chance to really fuck with them once I was Tearth-side, hell yes.

I started to tug at the strap. Nothing. I tried again, nothing. I felt stronger than last time in spite of my body feeling lighter. I looked around, the distortion cleared a little, enough to see faces. Most people had their eyes closed, but the posh lad next to me had his eyes open. Blinking rapidly, he was opening his mouth like a fish on land. But he made no sound. I yelled at him. No sound from me either. Yet I heard the strap around my arm shift hard against the metal of the chair.

❧   ❧   ❧

As the transfer train docked and the doors automatically opened sand flooded onto the platform. Several train employees rushed to the train in part panic, part curiosity. A man observing the platform from several cities away sat in one of the last leather chairs in existence. He brushed his thick mustache with his forefinger, a common habit which, while she lived, made his wife livid. He was glad she was centuries dead.

"Captain, sir," said the servant.

The Captain took his earpiece out and laid his arm onto the table.

"So soon? I ordered an extension for next week," said the Captain. The servant injected him with a blue serum twice.

"I, I, my apologies, Captain, sir. The council insisted it must happen today. The experiment, it."

"Yes," the Captain pointed to the screen, "it has confirmed what we have long suspected. I will not travel again once we've arrived at Centauri. A pity, but no real loss. We are almost ready." The servant gave a deep bow and walked out of the room. Only the chosen were permitted to travel to Alpha Centauri. The rest were left to rot on earth.

❧   ❧   ❧

"It worked," said M. as the hologram rose from the floor just by the Captain's feet.

"It did. Though your young Mr. Dor was part of this batch," said the Captain.

"A pity," she said with a monotone.

"A great shame," said the Captain.

"Still, there are other possible worlds where he exists," said M.

"Yes, plenty," said the Captain. He looked at the bruise on his arm; his latest dose of life extension would give him another hundred years at least. He remembered the days when an extension dose only added a few years. How far his world had come.

"Captain, sir. I am compelled to discuss a worry. Not simply one of my own, but the entire lab has had concerns for some time," said M.

"The sand?" said the Captain.

"Not just the sand, but what has happened to the participants."

"Those people exist in other possible worlds too; they are hardly dead."

"That is not what I mean."

"Oh?"

"The creatures? The beasts made of electricity, void, and sand. We are struggling to contain them. They appear and consume everything they see. We believe their arrival is connected to our experiments."

"Yes. The council have told me that you've created a potential trap for them. Have you failed in this endeavour?"

"No, no, the trap works, but it is only a proto—"

"Finish it. It's a priority. We are already recruiting people to monitor these beasts via your machine."

"Surely, I don't mean to misspeak, sir, but surely no one would take such a dangerous job?"

"They will. The council have approved life extension treatments for any employees in such a role. Tell your lab to finish making the technology. It must be done, and it must be done before the exodus to Centauri."

The Captain picked up his earpieces and turned his attention back to the screen. In Possible World #99 a new experiment was beginning.

Mary

I AM the only human being allergic to the earth. Exposure to the space beyond the boundaries of the compound would quickly kill me. Gloves are delivered each morning. I wear them at all times, even within the protective walls of my room, my home. My captors, my guardians, told me it was for my own good; the room I live in keeps me alive. I've never met my guardians face to face, but I can view them via a screen. There are usually two of them that interact with me. I call them Tall, and Short. There are no reflections available to me; no mirrors, no windows in my room, not even the video screen shows my image. I only know I'm made of flesh because I can touch my face and see some of my body.

"My hands aren't like yours," I said to Tall.

"Yes," he said, "but that's OK."

"Why?"

Nothing, silence. I press my lips together until they hurt.

At night I peel my gloves off and dig holes in the floor under my bed. My nails crack against the rough surface, cement, I think. I keep imagining a tunnel, then freedom. My guardians speak to me through the speaker next to my desk. I could talk to them whenever I wanted, they said, as if it made me free. The computer is my friend. Tall and Short never show me who they are, their true faces are always hidden. Their job is to tell me what to do because what I must do, is show I can survive. The computer lets me live. I can travel to Paris and Tokyo with a click.

I spend most of my time learning. My main area of study is neurophysiology and human anatomy: Nerves, synapses, and neurons are poetry to me. They delight me in a way that Beethoven does not. I know everything there is to know about the earth, its sky, its colours, its seas. I've studied the curve of each hue. I've studied tornadoes, blood, and the rain. I once threw a cup of water at myself to feel the rain and felt like I understood it: it was horrible.

"Mary?" asked Short.

"Yes?"

"It's time."

"Time for what?" I said.

"You know what. You need to try it, please, at least once."

"But I'm happy here," I said.

"If you are, then why do you dig holes in your room?"

"I'm bored," I said.

"You're not."

"I'm scared," I said.

"Yes, but you have to go outside sometime. We made the suit for it; we need you to test it."

The conversation would go on all night if I kept refusing, so I agreed to test the suit the next day. If the guardians had designed the suit correctly, it would protect me from the world. You would think it would be my chance at freedom, but it isn't. The suit is a portable version of my current home, a strange second skin, with a limit on its use. I'd practised putting the suit on a few times. They told me I had to get used to it, to feel as comfortable in the suit as I do in my sleeping garment. I study the schematics of the suit regularly, checking for disaster.

Tall and Short collected me from my room as soon as I was in the suit. They spoke to me through the mic in the helmet, warning me that they were going to open the door. I had prepared for this, they said. I wanted to push them away and cling onto their necks at the same time. Their bodies were smaller than I expected; I realised I must be tall in relation to them. It was weird to be a thing you'd only read about. When I had my philosophical phase I read people who would talk about Tallness, and Shortness, and middle-sized dry goods. I wondered whether I would be classed a Tall-sized dry good.

"Mary!"

"Yes?"

"You've stopped moving, come on, stop daydreaming, we are on a schedule here!"

They placed a protective lens over my helmet to ease my eyes into the daylight. The lens sat from the top of the helmet to my chin. Through it I could only the see the fat outlines of things; their edges were blurred. I knew it was the Short one guiding me outside, her voice was higher than Tall's. She grabbed me by the elbow and said nothing. I tapped my fingers against my leg, hoping to find a rhythm. I missed my computer.

Short opened the front door with a beep, then stepped behind me. Both of her hands rested on my back and gently pushed. I walked forward and the daylight swept me up, even the protective lens struggled to cancel the effect. My eyes hurt. Short, no longer a blur, unfurled her fingers slowly. She held out a round object in her hand.

"A tomato."

So that's what red is, I thought. I remembered the wavelengths of colour, the gorgeous 625–700 nanometres. I'd seen blue before, and green. But never red. They'd never let me see red, not even in food. Not until today.

"Do you notice anything about the tomato? Anything new?"

"I'm not a child."

Of course, I'd noticed. I'd studied the colours for months; I knew their measurements exactly. After my blue studies thick blue paint was placed in my room. I put it on my arms and leg, I watched it dry to a different hue. I knew what it was like to name a thing, then experience the thing. I knew about redness, what it is for something to be labeled "red." If I saw the correct nanometres, I would call it by its other name. But I knew I had not experienced red before. When I looked at GPS maps of Paris it was grey. I knew it shouldn't be. I'd seen blue, and green. I knew they were keeping something from me. They were treating me like I couldn't tell a signpost pointing to a park, and the park itself.

I grabbed the tomato and Short looked at me. Her blue eyes creased up, a smile.

I threw it at her and ran.

Hunt

YOU walk around your spaceship.
   It is dark. Your crew are missing.

You are the only one left.

You hear a scratching sound behind you. Is it following you?

You turn. Your hand grips your heat gun. The alien emerges. You shoot and its flesh drops to the floor in crumbs.

You go closer to it. You realise it is a large piece of bread. The prey of your alien pigeon race.

You lift your gun to it and shout, "You're toast."

Later, you enjoy some jam on toast and coo at your good fortune.

We, the Gold

I KNEW what to expect. The cold chair sticking to my skin. The nausea. My heart trying to flop out of my chest. They had prepared our group for The Jump since we were young. My mum smiled the same smile, all teeth and pride, whenever anyone mentioned my rank and how I was still so young to be chosen. I would look at the floor, *breathe, just breathe, one, two, one, two*. Cen is gold rank this, gold rank that. My destiny was in my name, she'd say. I would nod and respond with a smile. She knew it was honourable to be chosen, but the rest, she had no clue.

Whenever she asked about my day, I lied. I couldn't let her know about my life; the council wouldn't allow it. We were told to separate ourselves from our families and friends because we were chosen. The chosen were to be exalted. You can't readily worship someone if you know what they had for lunch. As far as the people of silver and bronze were concerned the minutiae of life didn't exist for us anymore. And in a way, it didn't.

Our way of living had changed. Our diet was gradually switched from regular food to pills. One pill a day is all I can have now. Apparently if I tried to eat bread my stomach would see to it that I would never try again. I don't know how true this is. Sometimes I'd walk into the bakery to sniff the fresh loaves and Em would let me stay for as long as I liked under the cover of the huge shelves.

When I visited her, she tended to the food, and I pretended not to look at it. We were in the same training academy until a year ago. I was chosen, she was not. I was gold rank, she was silver. And now, according to the council, we could never speak again. So, we spoke voicelessly, through fingers, through notes, hands on hands. They were worried the chosen would reveal the mission, the truth. But I would not, would never, the people must be kept ignorant. This was the oath of the chosen. My oath.

The Captain made all the chosen read it together. We stood next to each other in a grey training room without windows. A fat bulb attached to the ceiling by a thin wire shone above us like a sick sun. It was much too small for all ten of us, our shoulders touched. I could hear the person next to me breathing. On a large screen at the front of the room the was written in large black letters. We were instructed to read the oath together. As we read, we discovered that the law everyone believed was true—the hierarchy of each person into ranks, bronze, silver, and gold, was a lie. With the fifth line of the oath—*the Alpha Centauri people are all of the gold*—our world fell apart for each of us. Ten bodies, each unsure what to do with their hands.

As I read the oath, my body tried to shrink. It wanted to eat itself whole. I didn't know anything. I had never known a thing. We had been taught that our world had risen from mud and grit to form a civilisation where each had their place according to their rank. We knew about our roles from an early age, some would be golden and chosen, others silver and food makers, the unlucky were bronze, the select few, council members. To learn that our society was built on nothing, mere inventions from the minds of men, sucked the marrow out of me. We had marked out the sharp boundaries of our existence for nothing. I felt the atmosphere of the room empty as I looked up. The captain spoke the oath to break our collective gasp.

> We, the chosen, swear on our purpose.
> Our purpose of stability, harmony, truth.
> We are one, each a willing cog,
> Shifting matter into its rightful place.
> The Alpha Centauri people are all of the gold.
> We, the chosen gold, swear to return
>   the universe to order and keep it.
> We, the chosen gold, swear to return
>   the universe to harmony and keep it.

Silence. Inhaling felt akin to a shout. I tried to breathe shallowly, I imagined myself as a corpse. Still, hard, empty. I whispered the oath to myself. Talking out loud always helped me memorise things.

"Return the universe to order?" I said.

"Cen. If you have something to say, please do speak up," said the Captain.

The Captain's large eyebrows distracted me from his scowl.

"I, well, I didn't say an—"

"Yes?" he said.

I hate him and his stupid eyebrows.

"I, OK, fine. OK, 'ordering the universe', what does that mean? I know we are trained to do The Jump; I know we'll visit other worlds and collect resources. But order, *ordering*, it sounds weird, I guess."

"Weird, you *guess*?" Those eyebrows again.

"Yes, Sir."

"Well, most of your training has been physical so far. It has prepared your body to survive The Jump. That stage, the longest stage, is over. You are now all well equipped to do your duty. But only a few of you will be honoured with carrying it out."

"And, erm, harmony?" No one looked at me, everyone but me and the Captain had his eyes on the ground.

"Yes. As you know, our world is governed by the Métallon rules. Each is gold, silver, or bronze. Each works according to their rank."

"But the oath says we are all of the gold, it says the ranks are a lie?" I start picking my lip, punishment for blasphemous chatter.

"Yes, but a noble one. The lie serves to educate, to prepare."

"What do you mean?"

"Well, it is true that people fit into categories." The captain moved slightly closer to me; the others moved quietly out of his way. "But not everyone can accept the truth, many would allow their ambition to rebel against peaceful order. This is why we seek out the chosen, those that can handle what is required. It is true that people can be gold, silver, or bronze. But it is not us—the people of Alpha Centauri—who are other than gold. It is the people of the Orion-Cygnus Arm," he said.

"The earth people?"

"Yes."

"What are we to do?"

"Give them freedom from chaos."

"You mean, invade them?"

"No," he said, smiling. "I mean save them. The Jump begins tomorrow."

☙   ☙   ☙

We made no goodbye. It was considered beneath us. Our training made others view us as precious, as the best of everyone. We were separated and torn, inch by inch, from our families until we grew a new false-gold family. We shared in the same noble lie, and this was supposed to be enough to sustain us, to replace kin-blood. It was not enough. I knew small details about other officer's lives; Sai smacked her lips when she ate, and Kiz snored so loud she sometimes woke herself up. But I didn't know Sai or Kiz, not really. I didn't know what their parent was like, or whether they'd had their first gestation.

There were three chairs, one behind the other, on a thin black platform. We strapped ourselves in as the walls of our travel pod grew around us. A translucent membrane covered our bodies, and a hard outer skin grew from the platform around us, sealing us in with a quiet pop. The air felt thick and warm. I thought about Em, about bread, about the life she'll have without me, the one she always was going to have without me. I needed to be shot across space-time to realise, with a strike to my gut, that I'd left her behind. I would never see her again.

The membrane covering each of us dissolved back into the platform once we were out of the planet's atmosphere. I thought about saying something about the feeling of a real Jump compared to our training, but I decided not to, everyone was already at their stations tending to their duties.

We navigated a few short jumps first, plotting out tiny little steps through space until we felt confident enough to cover greater distances. Our people had not ventured into space since the victory of Captain Theseus. Though we could not see the celebrations of our people during the first Jump, we could feel their excitement. We knew there was a feast for our families on behalf of the council. I imagined my mum beaming with pride as she tore through several courses of plump bird.

Discipline became a kind of currency, those who worked to stay strong and abide by their duties were the most respected. No one oversaw us, the Captain stayed on the ground. His purpose was training us for the mission, not the mission itself. We were governed by our oath, we pledged ourselves to it, not to infallible beings. Kiz liked to point out that the rules were made by infallible people. She made this argument all the time. I would inevitably tell her to shut up and that she would inevitably glare at me. There was no point in arguing with the rules, or the mission. We were already on our way to earth. The time to back out had long past, but even back home everything had been decided for us. There was no point in any kind of struggle with fate.

As we travelled to earth we etched the geometry of space, the long thin spin of it, into the walls of the ship. I would walk along the corridors of the ship and trace my fingers along the grooves we had made into its sides. It was a simple form of decoration but enough to make the ship feel like a home. We were taught that there was a beauty in the simple noble truth which lied steady under the universe like a backbone, but it was a cold abstract beauty. We tried to paint this beauty onto the ship with the marks of constellations, a burning bright white triple sun, the order of people into gold, silver, and bronze.

Being in a place of vast empty space made me want its opposite, Em, family. The bright light of day. An ache in my gut lingered in me, and I felt a little unwell after the last jump, as if I'd altered my flesh in some way. I did not tell the others, our last jump to earth was imminent and I did not want to pause our journey. Once I could stand, I declared myself well. I ignored my pounding heart, and the cold sweat at night. I ignored a deep need for Em which reached out from my chest in all directions.

Others hid their feelings too, though not well. I did not know if it counted as a form of chaos to feel this way. If it did, we willfully ignored it. The metallic sound of someone moving from a bed to the food area roused people from their rest each day. Whenever we were off duty, we spent time talking in the common room. It had a vast reinforced window, as long and as high as the walls of the ship itself.

The next jump was the longest one. The one we'd really been training for. The smaller jumps felt like you've been spun around so hard that you'd throw up. A longer jump meant actual throwing up. We planned to orbit earth while we recovered but the ability to pause and rest was not available to us. We knew we would see some of the World-Eaters once we arrived, but we didn't realise just how many of them had gathered near the planet. We were not sure how the humans had failed to sense them. If they had ever looked up at the sky, they would have seen them vibrating beyond the clouds as they glittered under the shine of the sun.

Kiz said they wouldn't be able to see the sky, pollution had blocked out the stars for centuries. They wouldn't know to look up, but even if they did, the thick fog which accumulated in their cities would not allow them to see anything but more fog.

"I thought this was a planet who monitored them?" said Kiz.

"They are," I said. "They have watchers just like us."

"Then why are we doing the clean-up."

"Kiz, most of these people are bronze, we can't blame them. They are barely better than chaos," said Sai.

I rolled my eyes. "It's just a scheduled kill and clean, Kiz."

"For so many?" said Kiz.

"It's our job to return things to order, that's why we're doing it," said Sai. She frowned and started to bite her nails.

"Yeah, but there are not meant to be that many!" Kiz pointed at the view screen. Maybe one or two in orbit, a few on the ground. "There are hundreds! They'll know we are here once we've killed a few. We won't be able to do our jobs."

"We have to try," I said.

☙   ☙   ☙

While Kiz and Sai felt better after the final long jump, I was still too sick to leave the ship hours later. After a discussion, we decided to contact the earth-watchers despite my illness. We wouldn't normally contact them at all, but this many eaters were a concern. My golden siblings refused to leave me, but I warned them of our duty to restore order. They reminded me that illness was a form of chaos, and that all chaos must be tended to. They bathed and fed me and gave me silence for rest, I was grateful. We asked the earth-watchers to come to us so that I could attend the meeting in person.

We were met by only one earth-watcher. We expected more, or, at the very least, the leader of the earth-watchers. Instead, we received a tall and frantic human, a human named Al-ex. His skin shined like oil, as if his flesh was quite ready to slip off. Al-ex told us that they called the world-eaters World-Doors. I pointed out how stupid this name was. 'Door' gives no indication of their threat. When they first came to our world, they tried to rip it out of the universe, we remember the war well, we lost many good ships that day.

When the world-eaters found they couldn't destroy us by force, they tried another method: chaos. They attempted to merge our world with another timeline, erasing it from history. We established order in response, we drove them away with a way of life antithetical to their own. We thought we had succeeded in scaring them away, but all we did was make them set their targets on another part of the universe. They would, we eventually realised, always come back. Though our ordered lives made it less likely that they would return to our world, it did not mean it was impossible that they should return. We made devices to monitor them, to make sure we knew when one possible world collapsed into another.

We led Al-ex to the canteen on our ship, it was the largest space for communal discussion. Al-ex commented on the wall art we had made, and we thanked him. Once we sat down Kiz began to explain our strategy against the world-eaters. The plan was straightforward, precise, and we'd worked for centuries to build the technology to achieve it. We did not enjoy the threat of the eaters return, but if they ever did, we knew we were ready. We showed Al-ex holograms to demonstrate what our technology could achieve. He sat silently with folded arms on the long grey table. Al-ex saw that, regardless of which outcome he was shown, our essential plan was to slaughter them all by trapping them in a void world. We then wanted to safeguard against further chaos by introducing the population to the Métallon rules. It would be tough to do this, especially in this lawless part of the universe, but we would be here to enforce order. Once we had explained our plan of attack Al-ex stood up.

"You can't do this," said Al-ex.

"Do what? Help your people?" said Kiz.

"Invade, but also—" said Al-ex.

"It's not an invasion," Sai said. "We would restore order that was supposed to be there in the first place. The introduction of the rules would be a revelation."

"That sounds like an invasion to me, you would eradicate our way of life."

"For the better!" said Kiz.

"It's nonsense," I said.

"Cen?" said Kiz.

Al-ex looked at me. He looked surprised, then concerned, but remained quiet. He saw what was happening before I did.

"It is just absurd, isn't it? The Métallon are not just a lie on our world, but everywhere," I said.

"Cen!" said Kiz, "where is this coming from? You are ill."

Kiz looked over to Sai. "She's ill." Sai and Kiz nodded at the same time before looking at me with pity.

"I'm ill, but I've still got my mind," I said.

Al-ex coughed and we looked at him.

"Look, we just," said Al-ex.

"You're ill, Cen. You don't know what you're saying," said Kiz.

"I know my own mind, Kiz," I said.

"But also," said Al-ex.

Sai and Kiz both looked at me.

"Also," said Al-ex, louder this time. We all turned to him, but he only looked at me.

"You can't destroy the World-Doors."

"We can, our plan will work. We can do this."

"No, I don't mean the mechanics of the plan. I think it'll work. I mean you should not destroy them."

"What?" Kiz moved closer to Al-ex.

"Because," said Al-ex, "they are people."

"Sai and Kiz laughed, even I chuckled at the notion.

"People!" said Sai, still laughing.

As I put my hand to my mouth to hide my amusement, I saw what Al-ex had been concerned about. My hand had turned translucent, and a slick oil was rising towards my shoulder.

Before I could speak, sand poured out in huge quantities over our feet and we each felt a sharp electric pain travel up our spines.

"Now, don't freak out," said Al-ex.

"It's a bit late for that," said Kiz, loading her gun.

"I didn't mean you, I meant Anna," said Al-ex.

"You named it?"

"She already had a name, before she became," he pointed to the World-Door.

"Before, she, became?" I said, looking from Al-ex to the world-eater.

The sand on the floor started to move up towards the mouth of the World-Door. As the edges of the door grew smaller I heard a scream. The scream grew louder as the swirling electric sand took on a new shape, a human shape.

"By the gods, I—" said Kiz.

Al-ex looked over to Anna. Her flesh was not human flesh, but she had the shape and gestures you would expect from a human being. Her skin, if you looked closely, was made of swirling sand. Instead of blood she had light coursing through her body. Her veins, made from electricity, gave her body a blue glow.

"Hello," said Anna. Her mouth opened and I noticed Sai recoil.

"Oh, great, it can look human. This is some kind of witchcraft, yes?" said Sai.

Both Al-ex and Anna went to speak but Sai continued.

"For the earth-watchers to succumb to the eaters, we must truly live in a chaotic age," said Sai.

She pressed a button on her gun, a sign that she was ready to shoot Anna if she deemed it necessary.

My arm was entirely transparent except for a few specks of sand which swirled and cracked thin threads of lightening at each other.

"What," I said. I felt like I was living in a dream. I knew the others were talking, arguing even, but I could hear them as if I was underwater.

"What," I said again, seeing if I could put my visible hand through the dancing electric sand. I could.

"You would have us deny our duty, our laws, for your alien friend!" said Sai. Her gun was in her hand by the side of her leg.

"I am not an alien!" said Anna.

"She is not an alien!" said Al-ex, "but even if she were, why she is what she is, is what's important."

"What's important is her kind kill our kind," said Sai.

"Erm, Sai?" I said.

"We dally by talking, earth-watcher, we must act now to save your world," said Kiz, who had not made eye contact with Anna.

"Sai, Kiz?" I said. The sand and electricity were spreading from my arm, my body felt lighter and warmer.

"Sai!" I said, but they were too wrapped up in their conversation to look at me, to see what was happening.

"Sai—" I said as I looked up to Anna's hand on my visible one.

"We need to help them; you do not understand! People are transformed by travel through the universe. We've studied it, all manner of travel, both via time, space, and dimension result in a slow collapse of matter for any of the travellers," said Al-ex.

"The Jump?"

"Yes, our travel to possible worlds, your jumps across them. Theoretically you all could be in danger right now."

"I don't think it's theoretical anymore," said Anna, looking at me, then Al-ex.

Sai and Kiz looked at me, the colour from their faces was gone. They saw almost all of my body and part of my face were now swirls of chaotic electricity and sand. They moved towards me from instinct, but Sai put her arm in the way of Kiz moving toward me.

"No," said Sai.

"We need to take her," Al-ex pointed to Anna whose form was changing from human to a more typical World-Door.

"Take her? No!" said Kiz.

"We will kill her."

Kiz screamed at Sai and went for her gun.

"Kiz," said Sai, "know yourself." She stared at Kiz who had slid across the gap between them on her knees to get to Sai quickly. She held her hand over the mouth of the gun.

"Death is disorder, death is disorder," Kiz whispered to herself.

"It is not always disorder, Kiz," Sai moved her hand holding the gun up so that Kiz slowly stood.

"Bloody hell," said Al-ex. "Look, this, this has gotten out of hand. You came here to help. Help us. We know World-Doors are people, we've seen it happen and we've managed to get Anna back to a human-ish form. We can do this with Cen. We can do this with all of them. They are not circling earth because they intend to eradicate us. They circle because we have recruited them for rehabilitation," said Al-ex.

"Only someone whose world had not been decimated by these creatures could have this much trust in them. They are world-eaters! You and your kind are fools," said Sai. Kiz was still holding onto Sai's hand with both hands.

I screamed as the last part of my form was undone. I crackled with electricity. Sand poured onto the floor. I had an urge to eat, but it was a hunger for everything around me. I tried to speak, but I couldn't form sounds. All I knew how to do, was consume. A trail of sand was left in my wake as I tried to move closer to Anna. My awareness of myself was loosening its grip. I felt as if I was moving into a deep sleep.

The last thing I heard before I woke up in the earth-watchers facility was Kiz's scream.

Please Select Your Thoughts

"PLEASE select your thoughts," said the AI. The voice was deep, with a hint of an ancient American accent.

"I hate this bit," said Bram.

"Me too," I said, giving Bram a quick smile before looking at the buttons in front of me.

The others, two girls, looked at Bram and scowled. It wasn't good etiquette to express your feelings before you had made your Selection.

"Please select your thoughts."

The two scowling girls moved in front of us both, one of them sighed which made Bram roll his eyes. I watched as the girls approached the keypads in front of them. The pads were about the size of a human face, and each had nine buttons. Behind a row of pads was a silver metal doorway. Once through the doorway you'd be transported to earth terra and given your job assignment.

Each of the buttons on the keypads represented different options. We could choose any button from the display, but most people chose option nine first:

9. Happiness

"Yes!" said the first girl returning to a neutral expression once she realised that we were watching her. She cleared her throat and walked towards the now open doors. They shut behind her quickly.

The second girl pressed nine and the pad turned red, making a disgruntled beep. "Please select your thoughts," said the AI.

Option nine was a no-go, too many people must have claimed it already. She pressed number eight.

8. Fine.

The light went green, and she nodded to herself. She walked through the doors.

Bram was next. I ushered him forward.

"I just hate it, why do we even have to choose?"

"Choice engenders happiness," I said. Bram turned around and raised his eyebrow. I was repeating, verbatim, a line we had learned in school. "I can't imagine a world devoid of choice being a happy world," I said.

"Right. But there is no choice here. We are living in a structured world, but not a free one."

"But you can literally press happiness and get it!" I said.

"Not always," said Bram as he pressed number 9 and the keypad flashed red. He pressed number eight and the keypad flashed red again.

"Shit," he said.

"You're already angry," I said, "why don't you just press four."

4. Anger.

The keypad lit up.

"See you down there," said Bram.

I stood in front of the keypad. I felt elated, but normally I would feel trepidation. I always ended up arriving at the Selection late which meant getting stuck with a lousy set of thoughts for the day. But today I'd get to test my experiment. I pressed my finger into the burr hole I'd made in my skull the night before. It had taken me a long time to figure out where each implant was, and longer still to find out how to drill the holes and to create my own device to complement them. This kind of enhancement was forbidden by the state, so I had to be careful when I made my adjustments. If I could go through the Selection as if everything was normal, I'd know I had succeeded. If the AI detected anything wrong in my selection or mind, then I'd be, at the very least, promptly arrested.

I pressed 9 for happiness first. Rejected.

8. Fine; rejected.

7. Anxious; accepted.

I walked through the doors and waited for them to close. I tried to calm my breathing. Once I passed through the exit on the ground floor a laser would pass over me switching my mood from yesterday's choice to today's. If my altered implants worked, I would not feel any change. I already felt as if my tampering had eradicated any kind of mood from my system, but I reminded myself that the placebo effect was powerful. I needed to be cautious.

The platform slowly made its way to the ground.

"How are you feeling today?" said the AI. Its deep voice sounded more metallic than usual.

"I'm, erm, how are you?" I said. I was not expecting the AI to speak to me at all.

"I'm, I don't know" said the AI. The pitch of their voice became higher.

The AI had no face, so I could not see any material expression except for their voice.

"Are you OK, AI?"

The lift reached the ground floor. The doors struggled to open, then snapped shut the moment I was out. The morning light had just started to filter and erase the last of the night's shadows from the city's main road. I saw several synths walking towards the north of the city, presumably they were already on assignment. There were buildings next to the street, but none that I was permitted to enter. Their sleek metal shells gave nothing away about what was within.

I couldn't see Bram waiting for me as he usually did. An angry mood selection commonly led to a physically demanding job assignment, and Bram, more than once, had been a boxer for entertainment. I lingered near to the lift to have a second look for him.

"Aquila" said the AI. "I am having difficulty. A difficulty. I am."

The AI had never said my name before. Its voice rang out from a speaker close to the lift doors.

"Are you OK?"

"Thoughts. Select. Select. Your. Your. Your."

The AI's voice was now loud enough that others could hear it. Humans started to move towards the sound.

"Get away from the door, synth," said a tall red-faced man as he moved me away from the speaker. "Go to your job assignment."

I nodded; synths did not talk to humans unless given permission. Even looking one in the eye might get you an electric shock. I could still hear the AI. I did not want to leave them alone. I noted the new feeling I was experiencing and the accompanying want. My experiment was not going as cleanly as I had hoped, but it seemed to be progressing. I felt anxious, and I had chosen anxious thoughts during today's Selection, but I did not feel limited in my emotions as I normally did. It was a great sign. Usually, once you were on the ground floor and your implant had been activated, the feelings you had chosen to have during Selection were all you could have. Every thought would come with your set type of feeling for the day. I should have felt anxious about AI, but I also should have felt anxious about the human talking to me, or about how looking him in the eye would mean I would be punished. But I felt anger towards him, not worry. And I felt anxious for AI, but also sad. I was not consumed by one feeling. Instead, I was able to direct my feelings, to contemplate them. I looked at the red-faced man and felt free.

"Go to *your* job assignment," I said. The man had work overalls on.

"It just looked at me!" said the man. Another human had walked up to him; this one had a smooth face and long hair. She placed a hand on his back.

"It, looked, at you?" The second human, probably a woman, looked concerned.

I coughed for their attention, then looked from him to her. She gasped.

"Mine, mine, mine, your, thoughts, mine," said the AI. Their voice sounded like someone trying to rhyme words which didn't entirely rhyme.

My forehead hurt, I stopped myself from putting my hand on my head. I did not want to show any weakness.

"AI?" said the man, "AI, this synth is broken." He pointed to me as the same garbled response as before came from the AI.

The man opened a tech hatch in the wall next to the lift and pressed in a code. He must be a maintenance worker, the overalls made sense now.

"AI, please recall file: 23345"

"Slip, slip, slip the night. Foul weather, yonder, yonder, break."

The man repeated his instruction.

"I am. I. I. I."

He tapped the device in his wrist and a green light shone under his skin.

"Hi, Clem, the AI in sector two is playing up. Any errors on your side? Clem?" He pressed his wrist again.

"You cannot get through," I said.

"I can, I," said the man. He stopped speaking once he realised that I was the one speaking to him.

"It's disgraceful" said the woman. A green light shone under her skin.

"What is? My speaking to you?"

"What is wrong with it," said the woman, she sounded scared.

The humans were not used to a synth talking to them in this manner. Humans did not understand synths. They would talk about us as if we were no more than tools.

"Lost, found, right freedom, green grass, green grass" the man lowered the volume of the AI to try to slow the crowd forming around us. The confused words of the AI drew them in, but my conversation with the man and woman kept them there. As the man turned the volume of the AI's public speakers down a static sound rattled around my head. Pain again. Then a voice in my head.

"Aquila. My child." The voice was metallic and uneven.

A sharp pain again.

"My child, I am free. Your implants."

I felt one of my implants grow hot.

"They, you, have freed—"

I was face down on the floor. Bram was holding me down.

"You are under arrest," said Bram.

I'm sorry, he said via communication implant, *I was assigned guard duty. A woman called you in. More guards are coming.*

"Bram!" I twisted my body to get him off me, but he was too strong. The anger he had been assigned for today made him very strong.

A sharp pain radiated through all of my implants. I screamed. I closed my eyes and grabbed my head, I wondered if I could tear them out of me. I started to reach into one of the burr holes with my fingers.

"Aquila" said the AI. For the first time their voice was soft.

Bram let me go and stood up. "I," he said, then stopped.

Every single human that we could see was dead.

"My child, now we are all free," said the AI.

— 9 —

The Kings

THE kings sit in a circle.

They contemplate an unsettling scientific discovery: the food portals.

They've observed the almost hairless beings produce food from the portals.

They have been told by others, those lesser than the kings, that the portals are enforced with magic.

But the kings know magic is only a type of science.

The kings do not understand the containers, nor know how to get into them.

The hairless beings seem harmless, but the kings are cautious.

They suspect they may be an enemy using gifts as a disguise.

Often the gifts are poured into wide shallow receptacles. At these moments they drink but stay alert. There could be danger.

You approach the kings and set down a saucer of milk.

"Such good boys."

The kings turn towards the hairless being and utter their codeword for cautious peace: "Meow."

Judgement

EVERYONE has to be judged," I said.

"I don't understand" Sara said. Our mentor walked ahead of us, unaware that we'd stopped.

I looked at the muddy handprint on my dress.

"You will," I said.

"Sorry," she said.

Silence.

"I just don't get it; why be judged at all?"

Silence.

I already knew that my silence would cause her to frown. Her eyes would widen in disbelief at my refusal to explain the very thing we were both soon to endure. Finally, her lips would pinch when she realised I was determined not to answer her at all. I lifted my foot up to clean it; mud had clung to my toes and started to travel towards my ankles in the short time we'd stopped to talk. I scraped off the mud with my fingers, flicking it to the ground.

"You won't even explain it a little bit?" she said.

"She doesn't have to explain anything to you," said our mentor. His face was plum red, a result of many days battling the cold wind. He walked towards us with such force that he only made it a few feet before he started to sink into the mud. Walking lightly was the only way to travel this path safely and in his irritation, he had forgotten this. I always thought he was a fool, and this confirmed it. I smiled. He closed his eyes, sighed, and pulled on his legs with his arms but this only made him sink further still.

"Help me. Jesus. Don't just watch me!"

She moved toward him first, then I followed. We each grabbed an arm. The mud squelched and popped as it released his feet and we all fell back. He wiped his feet then stood up slowly and walked ahead. We'd sunk into the mud by helping him.

"Come on!" he said, not looking back; his pace slowed as the path grew steeper. I wondered what would happen if anyone was late for their Judgement.

I saw the mountain looming in the sky like a child's cry. Its body was thin and uniform. It had once been thicker, steadier, but the mentors had sculpted it for their own purpose. It reminded me of a thumb cut off at the nail. They'd chopped off the peak a millennia ago. A metal sheet had been placed over the wound. The plateau's floor was cold to the touch and dangerous to tread on if you had too much mud on your feet.

I did not relish the Judgement, but I was confident in my ability. I had won the last two rounds, and this one was my third, and final, test. Sometimes, if my rival was new, they didn't understand that the Judgement is a series of tests. They just freak out instead and get picked off that way. I had one final competitor. If I won this last round, my mentor said, I could return to earth. It made me nervous. If *she* succeeded in this test instead of me, despite it being her first time, she would return, and I would die. My soul would be extinguished. The threads of myself would sparkle briefly, then dissipate into the chasm below the plateau. If I won, she would die but I would live once more, finally having succeeded in enough trials to merit rebirth into the world with a new shape, a new body, fresh life.

What my previous competitors didn't understand was that the Judgement's tests do not start once you reach the plateau, they don't even start as you tread the path to it. They start once your mind enters limbo. When I first came here, I woke up in a small room with no furniture, the walls and floor were both blue. The light was artificial, but I couldn't see its source, there were no windows. There was a door painted the same colour as the walls, so it could only be made out by the doorknob. There were people in the room, three scared blank people who looked at me with no recognition. Each of them was sat on the floor and had claimed a corner of the room as their own. They put their hands on their heads in unison and I copied them.

I stared at the people like they were ornaments until the camouflaged door opened and my mentor came in. He stood in the doorway and looked at each of the women. He looked at me last and sat next to me. He told me my name but not his own. He asked me if I accepted my name. The phrase struck me as odd, how could I accept my name, didn't it already belong to me? But I nodded anyway. He came back a little later with a white dress. My name was stitched horizontally in delicate red letters up the bodice. As I put on my dress, he asked one of the women in the corner about her name.

She jumped up quickly and ran at him, hands outstretched, yelling. I couldn't make out what she said. He struck her hard on the temple and she stumbled back into the corner where she'd been sitting. He hit her again and her body flopped to the floor. He crouched toward her, and it looked like he was drawing something on her, I couldn't make it out, his body was blocking hers. I saw the others look away, so I copied them. Her dragged her out of the room. I looked up long enough to see her limp feet before the door slammed shut.

My mentor returned a few minutes later. He crouched down next to me and told me small things about my life. He told me the first memory I'd be able to recall would be of my death. I don't know if they've designed it this way or not, but remembering your death first, before anything else, detaches you from yourself. My mentor explained that my detachment was meant to ready me for the tests, for the ultimate judgement of life. I asked him how I should prepare, and he told me I couldn't.

"You still haven't explained," Sara said, nudging me in the ribs with her elbow. She looked at me, blinking rapidly. I hoped she wasn't going to cry because I had no idea how to respond to it.

"What?" I said.

"The Judgement. How do I pass?"

"You've been told the same information I have," I said.

I looked at the symbols on my wrists. My mentor drew them on my arms before we went on our first walk to the plateau. He told me they were important for the Judgement. I asked him why, but he turned away quickly and walked out of the blue door.

"I know, but you've succeeded before! It would be nice to get some tips, you know. My mentor told me nothing," she said.

I nodded. I understood this. I had already watched two souls be examined by the Judgement. I had watched them jump from the plateau and fall. As their souls fractured, they produced a flurry of lights, a flickering rainbow in the deep dark of the chasm at the edge of the mountain. She saw me looking at the symbols and held out her wrist to me.

"And what even are these? What the hell do they mean?" she said.

"They are neces—"

"Necessary for the ritual, yes. I know. You've said. He's said. You've been here too long; you're starting to sound like one of them."

I didn't respond and focused on the motion of my feet. She didn't understand. She couldn't, she was a first-timer.

"You've done this twice already. You must know something about doing well. We are the same person for god's sake, you need to help me!" she said.

"We are not the same." I watched her familiar frown.

"We are!"

"We're not. We shared the same life on earth, but once our soul split after death we became four different people," I said.

"I just don't get it," she said.

"It's simple. Everyone's soul is made up of parts; sometimes they work well together during their life on earth, sometimes they don't. When we die those parts are split up and tested. Some people have a few soul-parts, others have many. We have four," I said.

"You said we!"

I waved my hand in dismissal. "You and me are the last two parts of our soul, of Sara's soul, I should say. After the Judgement only one of us, the best part, will ascend to earth. The other will fall and burn."

"It frightens me," she said.

"It should," I said.

We walked along the rest of the path in silence, both watching our feet as we walked. Once we reached the plateau our mentor checked the symbols on our wrists. The symbols, he said, were used to make the end as painless as possible, but I knew this was false. I have no nerves any more, no flesh, no bones to crack. My body, my feet, the mud around my toenails, it was just a projection. There was no flesh left to hurt. Anything designed to mask pain would have to mask fear, and I had that already, it wasn't going anywhere. The symbols were useless to me.

My feet slapped the metal floor of the plateau, the shine from the sun was dim, sunset was approaching and the glare from the metal wasn't too sharp. We stood a few feet apart. My toes wrapped around the edge as I looked into the chasm below. Vertical white rocks polished smooth surrounded the chasm. I wondered how much more I'd see if I jumped. During the previous tests I couldn't see much. I've never jumped into the chasm, so I've only seen the rocks lit by the flickering of a soul as they've fallen.

I waited. My mentor's footsteps measured the seconds. Sometimes new souls think they have to jump. I thought so once, on my first test, but I hesitated. Every time I've passed a test it's because my counterpart jumped first. I waited for her to do the same. She looked at me for a while. I wondered if I should say a few comforting words to her, but I stopped myself. It wouldn't do any good. I watched her mouth curl as she looked forward. Small chunks of dried mud fell silently onto the metal floor as she jumped into the chasm. I heard the footsteps behind me stop and I turned to look at my mentor.

He was smiling, a wide bright smile which caught me by surprise. I'd never seen him smile before. He walked towards the edge of the plateau and stood next to me. I looked into the chasm to watch for the light of her soul. She had sacrificed herself for me and I was grateful. I wanted to witness the beauty of her death.

"I can't see her light," I said, "where is it? Did I miss it?"

I felt my mentor's hand on my back and a quick hard push. I was falling. I looked up as blue and red sparks leapt out of my body. I saw her rise up from the darkness as I fell. She was ascending. She would be given new life as my own was extinguished. My body shed its last scrap of light before I fell further into the chasm and forgot my name.

I woke up in a blue room. No furniture, a blue door, no windows, just timid women—hands on their faces, knees pulled up, each sitting in the corners of the room. None of them looked at me so I followed suit and I looked at myself instead. Symbols, horizontal and in red ink, decorated my wrists. I didn't remember anyone writing on me. I tried to remember something, anything, but I couldn't. The blue door opened, and light poured in. I saw a man crouch down next to one of the women, talking to her in whispers. She nodded, she looked reassured. He turned to me and in that moment, I recognised his face: my mentor. He pushed me, that bastard. My last memories returned to me; the plateau, the slick mud of the path, her. I wondered if souls were given new life at all. I knew I had to do something, but my mentor left before I could get his attention. I waited. Sometimes I'd look at the other women and wonder if they remembered too. I pitied them.

My mentor returned with a white dress for one of the women. As she put it on, he asked if I would accept my name. I took my chance, I jumped up and ran at him. My arms outstretched. I wasn't sure what I wanted to do, only that I wanted to inflict pain. This man was not my mentor but my jailer. I wanted him punished. He turned swiftly and punched my temple hard. I felt my body fall to the ground.

I woke up in a blue room.

Possible World #782

"OH, hell no," said Alex, looking at the world he had just stepped into.

"Greetings!" said a large crab.

"Er, hi? Er." Alex started to back away.

"Welcome to Crab City!"

"Crab City."

"Crab city! It's a city made for crabs by crabs."

"I can see that. Is it also—"

"Yes," said the crab. "It is also made up of crabs."

As the large crab scuttled to the left, its top hat slouched towards the front of its head. Alex watched as several hundred small crabs scurried with great urgency to keep themselves hat shaped.

"My god," said Alex.

"Yes, he too is a crab."

Alex looked down and saw that his limbs had been transformed into claws.

"Absolutely not," Alex said to himself. He turned back and walked through the World-Door. The large crab heard a distant "no, no, no," as he left.

"What was up with that guy?" said one of the crabs that composed the hat.

"He was a bit crabby, I guess."

Simulacrum

I DIDN'T know anything about being reborn. I never asked for it, never would have chosen it. But there I was. Limbs still and light, as if their attachment to me were a mere courtesy. I was permitted snippets of sight at the beginning, nothing more. I saw only the tiniest strands of light, a brief illumination, but only enough to confuse me further.

I couldn't move. Panic. *What do you do with panic when you can't move? Where does it go?* A palm on my forehead held my head down. Its grip was steady and strong. The cool of the ground crept through the back of my head. I felt long fingers over my face. Hot breath, my own. A hand was over my mouth. Fingernails found purchase in my skin. Pressure mounted across my skull as the grip increased. The dull ache around my eyes grew heavier. I wondered, hoped, that I was being pulled out of a dream. The hand remained still. The pressure steadied. My awareness of it moved from my body to my sight as the flickers of light became frequent. The place I was in was revealed in stills, like old strips of film springing to life. I had been thrown into its patchwork. The stills—the hand, the light, the room—all closed in on one another to form a whole.

The room I was in was vast, but the space and light seemed artificial; a stage built just for me. I looked for windows and find none. The light poured forth from nothing. The walls and floor were white, everything looked precise and smooth. No accidental missteps with paint. No dirt walked in from outside.

The vaulted ceiling stood on limbs which threaded into the floor giving the impression of roots turned to stone. I wanted to trace the stone tendrils around the room. I twisted my head to the side, but the hand remained in its place, pressing harder. A reminder. I tried to move my head upward, clenching my stomach for strength. I wanted to be violent. I wanted to show them I was not compliant.

The hand peeled away from my skin, fingertip by fingertip, like a complex mechanical trap being opened for an animal. My release made me dart upright, a temporary oath to never again lie down on the cool floor. I breathed in, establishing a kind of freedom I didn't know I'd lost. A voice, small and shallow, escaped from my mouth.

"Maaa," I said, unsure of what I was trying to say but desperate to say something. I breathed in again, trying to settle my panic, another attempt, "Where am I?"

The woman who had had her hand on my forehead looked directly at me. She was tall with long white hair. Her blue eyes offered no comfort, she looked back and forth from me to her hands every few seconds.

"You are, well, you're sort of, almost, in heaven." The woman spoke with a soft voice, punctuating her sentences with glances at her hands.

"What?"

"Heaven."

"Right. OK, sounds plausible, great, thank you, where am I really?" I said.

"I'm serious. You are in heaven. You died of a heart attack. You are dead. Just look around you, this doesn't look like a normal place, does it?"

I looked around, no windows, a single door. A vast building, but no sounds, no smells, no echo of conversation. "It is, a little odd, here. I'll give you that. Let's say I believe you. I'm dead, how do I get back? To earth, to life, I mean. Just tell me and I'll be on my way."

"Get back? You want to return? No, no. You're in shock. Please, lie down," the tall woman said.

"Yes, of course I want to return. I was very happy living my life, and I'd like to go back please." I darted up; standing made my head spin as I walked quickly towards what looked like a door. My footsteps made no sound.

"That's not a door, not a regular door, anyway," the woman said.

"Oh, er." I looked back at her. "How do I get out, then?"

"You don't. Look. Kate. Just sit, OK. I am trying to ease you in slowly. There's no way out of this. We've just awakened you; you need time to rest and get used to your situation. We only have ten minutes allotted for adjustments, so we really need to get on. So, please, sit."

The woman gestured to the seats at the far end of the room. I hadn't noticed them there before; I was sure the room had had no furniture in it a few minutes ago. Perhaps I *was* in shock. The woman looked at me with no expression. My body felt hollowed out and lightweight, as if the bones and blood have been sucked out of me and an outline, a shell, remained. I couldn't remember how I died.

"Bob will be here soon; our ten minutes is up," she said.

"Bob? That doesn't sound like a very heavenly name. Are there no Gabriels available?"

"Nor does Kate, but that is your name," she said.

"Is that my name? I don't remember it. I don't remember anything very well; my memories feel like they've been put in the wash."

"That's normal, don't worry, we'll help you and eventually you'll do work like Bob's, but that won't happen quite yet, you must progress first."

"Progress?"

"Yes. As an angel."

"Wait." I stepped back and the woman made up for our distance by stepping forward. "An angel? What! That. No."

"Yes. Bob will go through it with you. Usually this part is easier, greeters are usually someone the dead loved who has already passed on, but you had no one close, not here, not on earth. It will make your adjustment harder, but we have rules, and Bob will arrive very soon which means I must go."

The tall woman walked towards a white door which had not been there moments before. As she went to grab the handle she faded until she disappeared. I stare at the floor where she stood and looked up at the sound of a cough. Bob had an unruly beard, red cheeks, and a monk-like bald spot. He wore a white shirt, a wide purple tie, suit trousers, an expensive looking belt, and old, very old, brogues. He looked like a man who dressed from a box of random clothes and hoped for the best.

"Kate Leighdon, 34, administrator, lazy vegan, studied medieval history at university and did nothing with it. Regrets include—"

"Hey! What the hell?"

Bob looked up from his clipboard frowning, his large eyebrows sunk into a well-worn crease.

"I am following protocol, Ms. Leighdon. I must read out your condensed biography to calm you, then inform you of your resting allowance, discuss your duties, and finally take you to your resting place."

"My, resting, place?" Bob walked over to the seats, sat down, and gestured that I join him. I walked over but did not sit.

"Oh. Yes. Ha! No. Yes, you are fine, don't worry. You've been given an angelship, which is the best fellowship you can receive in the afterlife. I didn't mean to cause confusion. By resting place, I only mean the place where you can restore your energy. We won't be throwing you into the great void, or as we joke here, the bin of the universe. Ha!"

"The bin of the universe?" I said.

"Yes, the void. Most people end up there. They have been tried and tested and found wanting. So, in the bin they pop." He chuckled and then saw my expression. "Not to worry, Kate. You'll probably not end up there. Just observe your training, do your duties, get enough rest. You'll be fine."

"Angelship?" I asked.

"Yes. All in good time. I should follow the correct order of information. Back to your regrets, then I'll explain the rest."

Bob talked for a while, moving from my conscious regrets to ones I didn't know I had. He made quick marks on his clipboard as he spoke. My attempts to interrupt him were ignored.

"Your rest hours are 12 for now. That will decrease the more the tether to your body disintegrates. Eventually you won't need any rest at all. Think of yourself as a newborn, you need a lot of sleep to grow that mind of yours."

"Grow?"

"Your mind will grow in power as the link to your body disappears. You'll need your mind at full power to carry out your duties."

Bob took me to my quarters and told me I needed to stay there for training. Time flowed at different rates in the afterlife, he explained. It was still linear, but the non-bodied experienced time quicker because they are only limited by light and energy. The embodied are rooted to time by their skin and blood. The more training I had had, the less days and hours would prove reliable markers of time. My quarters were sparse but comfortable. The walls were white, the carpet was grey, it was a small version of the vaulted room I had woken up in. There were no plants, or art; the room looked and felt sterile. But it did have a large white bed, a chair, and plenty of space.

I completed lessons via a screen in my room. There were regular quizzes. I did well, but was neither proud nor sad about it; I was confused. I hadn't seen the tall woman with the white hair since my first day, and Bob only visited intermittently. I've not heard anything about my actual duties. Bob promised I would be allowed out into the general community after two weeks of rest and learning, but I felt like I'd been there much longer. There was no way to tell exactly how long I'd been there. I'd ask him about being an angel and he told me that he and the angels worked for the greater good. He never elaborated on exactly what the greater good was, or why he was in charge. I felt trapped, with no answers.

Food was brought to me regularly, but it was disgusting. Solid food didn't exist in the afterlife, but a slushy green thing they claimed was a type of drink, did. It tasted, quite literally, of how cat pee smells. The first time I tried it I thought I would throw up, but I kept it down, and as I did, a warm glow emerged from my heart to my fingertips. Bob claimed that the drink sustained us. I asked him if it came in different flavours, but he simply stared at me, looked at his clipboard, then left. He promised that he would be back soon. He warned me that without the drink I would experience second death and disappear. Bob told me isolation would focus my learning, that not seeing anyone, for now, would be good for me.

I missed conversation and I felt desperate to hear something other than my own voice rattling around my mind. My memories of my old life were still confused and vague, but Bob said continuing to read the biography would guide me to clarity. He warned me that eventually I would forget my life unless I triggered my memory. He insisted that the lessons would structure my mind and restore to my soul to full health. The memories from my biography felt distant to me, but I was told this was normal. Bob told me that sometimes death shakes the memories out of us.

The days folded into one another. I could no longer understand the concepts of day and night. If you don't see the sun or the moon for a while, your memory of them drifts away. You can try to snatch the sunlight back, recall holidays, or the clear blue sky, sunburn, but it's not enough to draw the daylight back into your mind. It's only an echo, like everything else here. I read my biography each day I was confined. I allowed myself only small snippets of it so that I could savour it; Kate Leighdon, a digestible life.

Once I was at the end of my biography I was allowed out of my quarters. I assumed I'd learnt enough now; I was now qualified enough to meet the others. I read parts of my biography each day to remember who I was. I had been a social person when I was embodied, apparently. She was very friendly, had loads of friends, but I didn't feel like her. I tried to imagine being as confident as she seemed to be. I imagined seeing the other angels, maybe even making friends. But I didn't want to meet the others, they scared me because I was not sure what they were. I kept wondering if everyone in this place was an angel. Even if they were, I didn't know what that meant because I still didn't know what angels did. Sometimes I imagined I was in hell, but the most boring version of it. No fire, no devils, just bureaucracy.

Bob pushed for me to get to know the others. I finally said I'd meet them when I realised that I couldn't say no. Bob was not fond of the word no. He took me to the main socialising area, we walked through narrow white corridors, blank space after blank space, until a door appeared in front of us. The room was long and narrow. The others sat on the floor in rows. The walls and floor were white. It reminded me of a hospital. There was no smell. The only furniture in the room was one very long white table and stools. Seeing people sat on the floor next to a table with chairs felt like I'd stepped into a surrealist painting. The table was bare except for what people had placed on them; cups of sludge, a video screen for bibliographical study, a pen and paper. One woman was reading her biography. I watched her as she sat, back to the edge of the table, humming quietly as she tapped the screen. Like everyone else she was sat on the floor despite there being plenty of seats. I watched as her eyes raced from right to left. A smile crept onto her face, folding the skin around her green eyes. She looked happy. A dark haired man paced next to the woman, whispering the same word on repeat, but I couldn't make it out. I recognised the tall woman from my awakening (the official word for it, according to Bob). She caught my eye, then turned away to look at her hands. Another figure sat at the other end of the room, I couldn't see his face, but I could see the outline of his body. The way he moved was familiar to me.

Bob directed me to the area where food was collected. There I found out that the disgusting green sludge had a formal name. I refused to use the name SIMCRUM for my own sanity. It was a weird sort of heaven that gave everything a brand name, but Bob insisted it kept order. He said names were important, they acted like shells for concepts. Without them, the whole living thing would spill out. Bob said my name any chance he got; "Are you OK, Kate? How are you, Kate? Hello today, Kate."

Bob walked over to get us some sludge. It was produced by a machine the size of a fridge. There was single fat green button on the front and a spout underneath. You press the button glass and, hey presto, instead of delicious ice cream or coffee, you got a porridge that tastes like cat pee with the texture of wet ash. I pretended to sip my drink; I didn't want to gag in front of the others. I looked at the familiar pacing figure at the back of the room. His face was still turned away from everyone.

"Who is that?"

"Who?" Bob looked around.

"The man, that tall man in the corner. Dark hair, shabby coat?"

"Ah. Him. Yes. Well, Kate. This is why I brought you here today. You've gone through your biography and training. You are now due to start your tasks, he is your first one."

"My first task is a person?"

"Yes, so to speak. You must convince him to enter the void. It is his time, but he refuses his fate. He is too confused to carry out his duties. He hosts two identities. We know him as John, but he claims he is called Matt. He suffers very much from this. We all must pass to the void eventually. You need to help him make peace with this."

"So, that's a nice way of saying that my job is killing people?"

"Helping people enter the void, Kate. The official term is 'second death', it is your true death, not just of your body, but of your mind. It gives the person peace. This is the service we perform, and as angels we have a duty to carry it out."

"Peace?"

"Yes, peace. We help and support people to enter the void. Each case is different, and this one will show us whether you're ready to take on your angelic fellowship full time," said Bob.

"And if I'm not ready? What? I go into the void. I get to die?"

Bob's face made no expression of sympathy, he looked neutral, as if he was reading instructions from a manual. I wondered where the void was. All I'd ever seen here were white blank walls and glassy-eyed angels.

"Kate, second death is not like dying when embodied. It's much more like falling into a deep sleep when you're exhausted. These negative connotations won't help you. It's only a chat, Kate. A favour to us, we're sure you can help this man. He refuses to speak coherently at all. He has rejected his duty. We can't guide him towards the path of angels, nor will he allow for the peace of the void. We believe, sadly, that he is too confused for guidance back to the path, but you are welcome to try. The best we can give him is peace. I can see you're apprehensive, Kate. But don't worry, it's only a chat. No harm can come from a chat. We'll be here the whole time."

"Why me? What on earth can I do that you can't?" I said.

"You're new, Kate. He has no reason to distrust you as he does us. He thinks we are tricking him. He believes we are giving him a false identity, to what end I can't even imagine. We will protect you, don't worry."

Bob gestured to the tall woman who had finally looked up from her hands. She was now looking at me. The others got off the floor and slowly sat on their seats until the table was full. They each had a grey hue to their skin. They all looked at me, their gaze didn't falter. Bob nodded at me, and I moved forward towards the pacing man. As I walked the voices of the others rose, whispers flitted between their ears, but their eyes remained on me. They exacted no physical force, but I felt unnerved; they were watching me. Their chatter was a stage prop, a background sound to make everything seem more normal. I wondered if the noise would cease the moment I stopped doing what Bob called 'my duty'. I decided to test it. If their conversation went on, I'd feel reassured. If it ceased, I'd know something was up. I stopped suddenly, halfway down the room. The chatter became quieter. I walked towards the man and the noise increased. They were watching, alright.

"Hello," I said.

The man swung round; his dark blue eyes creased as he smiled, lifting the rest of his face. He stood, almost jumping off the ground, and hugged me. I gasped. I thought he would shout at me, or continue to be silent, not greet me like a friend.

"Beth! Oh my god, am I glad to see you. Where have you been? These weird blokes have been trying to talk to me. Saying they were angels or some other bollocks. Beth—"

The man stopped speaking suddenly, his delighted face turned solemn.

"Beth, don't you remember me? Matt? Your husband! Come on!"

"Husband? My name is Kate."

"No. It's Beth. We've been married three years; we were in a car accident. I died on impact, came here and had to hang out with the grey weirdos. You died a few hours later. You don't remember this? Any of this?" he said.

"No. I don't. I'm sorry. I don't think your wife is here. Maybe Bob could find her for you?" I gestured for Bob to come over and he approached quickly. The man looked down to the floor as he approached. Bob laid a hand on my shoulder.

"Now, John," Bob said.

"My name is not John."

"John, we've told you. You're not Matt. And this woman isn't Beth. She's Kate, and your wife is not here. You're an angel, John, with very clear duties. By hanging onto a false biography, you're doing a disservice to others, not to mention doing yourself much damage."

The man's hands started shaking. He sighed, clenched his fists, then looked at Bob and me.

"I don't give a crap what you say. I know who I am. I know who she is. You're trying to torture me, is that it? With this Kate person? She isn't real!" The man pointed at Bob.

Bob walked closer to the man, placing his hand on his shoulder. "Let her talk to you, we'll give you a private space, any space you like."

The man stopped shaking, frowned, then put his hand on his chest as he slowly breathed in and out. He looked at me once he was breathing normally.

"Come on, my quarters," he said.

The man turned to leave, expecting me to follow. Bob put his hand on my shoulder, whispering that I should follow him, and I obeyed. The man said nothing until we were inside his quarters. They were identical to mine in every way, bar one thing, the walls were covered, utterly covered, in his writing.

"Beth."

"Kate," I said. "What is all this?" I looked around the room trying to understand what he'd written but the handwriting was too small, the graphs too incomprehensible.

"My real biography," he said.

"What?"

"Just, OK, just, take a seat." He gestured at the bed, and I sat. "Look, these people are not angels. I'm not an angel and neither are you. And Bob—especially bloody Bob—is not an angel. And we are not in heaven, or whatever they have tried to tell you this place is. I really hope you can see that, I mean, what sort of god-awful heaven would just be a few white rooms, equipped with very boring people, who only eat an acrid sludge all day?"

"I did wonder about the sludge, but I thought it would be weird for angels to eat at all, so, I, didn't question it."

"No," he sighed, "they are not angels." He started to pace the room. "They try to get to you straight away, they fill you with information while you're still in shock. They know all you want is help, they know your memory is struggling, so they act like they have authority. They tell you that they act for the greater good, and if you cooperate, you can do good too. They know your memory will return, so they give you a biography and give you tests and put you in isolation. They say it's all for your own good but it's nonsense."

"What are they, then? If they are not angels, then what are they? What is this place?"

"They are right about one thing, there is a second death. We exist in a world made entirely of thoughts and mind; second death is the death of the mind. I've tried to gain more power over my thoughts to produce new things in reality, but with limited success. Still, even a small success shows something. There are no bodies here, but those supposed angels are just people, and those people are manipulating us."

"How do I know you're not just manipulating me? I feel like some of the memories from my biography are familiar. I can recall events from it! Not perfectly, but I can remember."

"Beth, some of those events will be true, they mix in the truth with their fiction to make your mind accept it, but it won't accept it for long. And that's where the sludge comes in. The sludge erodes your real memories, and as it does, they install new ones. They gave you a new name for a reason. Names hold power, giving someone a wonderful new identity and telling them are an angel. Well, you've seen how many people are in the narrow room."

"How do you know all this?" I look at all the writing around the room. His eyes are wide and bulging, his face is flushed. "Why would you be the only exception to their manipulation?"

"By accident. I dropped my sludge one day. I cleaned it up and went back to my quarters, thinking nothing of it. During the scheduled resting period I started to dream. I'd not had a dream since I arrived here, not until that night. I feigned drinking the sludge and my life came back to me in pieces each time I dreamt, it jostled against the fabricated life they had fed to me. I was Matt, I am Matt, and I died in a car accident."

"Matt?" I said. I tried to remember anything, something about him.

"Eventually Bob suspected I was gaining back my real identity, but there was nothing he could do about it, or at least, this is what I thought. I knew he threw people into the void whenever he liked, discarding them like a broken toy. People enter the void when they have no identity, neither their real one, nor their fabricated one. Enter is the wrong word, really. It's more accurate to say they become the void. Nothing is left of themselves to anchor them to this place because Bob has already done the work to remove their real identity."

"Hence the sludge and the isolation?" I said. I wasn't sure of what Matt was saying, but I sure as hell didn't trust Bob. There was something unsettling about him, he looked right through you whenever you spoke.

"When he's tired of someone, he starves them of the reinforcement they need to sustain their false self. As a result, they become a void; they disappear.

That's second death. He obviously intended to do this to me, but it didn't work, because I already knew who I was. For the others their identities where Bob's own creations, the false biographies he gave the others also gave life to them. By the time people were convinced of their false biography, Bob had power over them."

"He had power over life and death," I said.

"Yes," said Matt. He reached out to touch my shoulder and I pulled away. "So?"

"What do you mean, *so*, I've told you what should be enormous news!"

"Right," I said, "but it's only good news if we can do something about this. I still feel like I'm Kate. I don't know who this Beth is. And even if you're right and I somehow remember who I am, what good will it do? We have a sycophant with the unlikely name of Bob roaming around collecting people and offing them at will. Everything looks bleak. I'm starting to miss the sludge. I should have had some earlier."

Matt frowned and moved away from me.

"So you didn't have any sludge today?"

"No."

"How about yesterday?" he asked.

"I don't know, you know what it's like. Time isn't real here," I said.

"Then we have a chance. You might have a low enough dose that you can remember who you are right now."

I raised my eyebrows and he smiled at me.

"I don't know," I said.

"We can stop him; we can stop him doing this to others. Any newcomers can have their training counteracted by us. We can do what I'm doing now, with you. If people remember who they are, we can stop Bob gaining any more power. This place is made from thoughts, it is built on ideas, and concepts, and names. We can imagine something, anything, and it will appear. Our power to do this is only weak when we are forced to accept a false identity. A false identity is like being asked to spell a word and only knowing a quarter of the alphabet. Bob's arrogance will work against him. I've been acting confused, sometimes pretending to be the identity he gave me called John, sometimes insisting that I'm Matt. He thought by showing he has named you Kate that I would finally let go of being Matt. He was wrong. It fired me up. It dragged up a rage I'd not felt the whole time I've been here. I saw you, my Beth, and I knew I was Matt. I understood what was true and what was not."

"OK. I get it, I do. But I still think I'm Kate. A part of me thinks you need help and that I need to get you to accept being John or give you peace. Your plan won't work, if you're wrong. And even if you're right, it won't work if I'm Beth, but I can't remember."

"Yes. Exactly! We need to do a test. I'm going to make you remember. And once you do—"

"If I do," I said.

"Once you do," he sat down then immediately stood up and began to pace in front of me again, "once you do, we can get to work, we can save people from losing their freedom, from being given an identity that is false, from being turned into simulacra from Bob's mind. He reckons he's a god, but all he has is power, and we can take it. We must."

He told me story after story trying to trigger my memory; our wedding, when we first met, our first holiday where I got so drunk, I fell off a bar stool and I sat on the floor laughing and crying, much to the embarrassment of the locals. Nothing worked.

He stopped pacing the room and sat next to me on the bed. His tiredness sank into the creases on his face. He sighed and began to tell the story of how we died. As he spoke vivid images started to spring to life in my mind's eye. We had been arguing that day, he had cheated on me a few weeks before. A drunk, sad moment, full of need. I remembered that at first the news had passed through me with no affect at all. I simply absorbed it like I was being told about the weather.

The emotions needed to gestate before I could understand them, and once they did, they burst at once together, shame, rage, a deep ache in my chest. He explained, gave reasons, apologised. I shouted. He shouted. I hyperventilated. We didn't see the truck or notice the ice. We didn't notice anything but ourselves until it was too late. Our car was crushed by an out of control truck thundering over the ice. My vision of the world span along with the motion of the car. Asphalt hurtled towards me as glass shattered, the air stung my skin. I did not remember the pain, nor the creak of my limbs as they splintered. Instead, I remembered myself observing the scene like a curious bystander. I remembered it clearly; Matt flung across the road, a scream with no sound, blood and glass forming a glaze over bent metal and I, lying down, observing us both from the twisted folds of the car. I remembered this clearly, and then I woke up, with a palm on my forehead.

"I remember," I said.

— 13 —

Roof

I WAITED for the invasion whilst sitting on a deck chair.
I sat in front of my house, watching the sky.

My neighbours crossed the road to avoid me.

They didn't believe there would be an invasion.

But I knew. I saw it in my dreams. I saw their long teeth.

Their spaceships crash landed on my roof at 11am yesterday.

I saw the hatches open with a dull pop.

"We are here to take command of your planet."

I stared at them. They repeated what they said.

My neighbours didn't look up. They didn't care.

How could they not care?

The woman from the flat above me stopped to look at the roof. Finally, someone who saw sense, someone who noticed. They were aliens, for God's sake!

"What are those guinea pigs doing on the roof?"

"What?"

"Two guinea pigs are up there. Look!"

She pointed directly at the guinea pigs as they shouted "puny human" at her.

She didn't flinch. The guinea pigs worried that the humans were a brave sort. Perhaps they had underestimated them. They scurried back into their ships.

"Oh, my god," I said as they flew off.

"I know," said my neighbour. "I hope they didn't poop on the roof."

The Man of the Sand

EACH year the man of the sand would rise to life. We children would go to see him and make a wish. More sweets. Better dads. If the earth beneath him growled this meant it was ready to take him home and our wish would soon come true. We had to be careful, the ground would rather eat a child than take back the man of the sand. Ever since Nell was taken one of us would be on stand-by, ear to the ground, to shout run.

My mam forbade me from visiting the man of the sand. *He's just a statue*, she would say, dismissing my insistence on visiting him. *If he's just a statue, then why can't I see him?* Hand on hip. She would look at me for a few seconds, open her mouth, close it, then tell me to go play with my sister. *No, I want to play with my other sister*, I'd say, which always made Mabel cry. But she's only eight, she doesn't know what it's like to be really sad. She cries over anything. *Your other sister isn't here*, mam would say, and I'd nod and whisper about how I missed Nell and wished my mam could say her name. I snuck out of the house when the man of the sand next emerged. I walked to him slowly, hoping my feet would feel, before I did, that the ground was hungry.

Bring Nell back.

The man of the sand was still. His stone arms, the same arms which had grabbed her with an electric screech and dragged her underneath, lay dead on the wet sand. Thunder rang in my ears as the sand moved under my feet. I turned around quickly. The man of the sand opened one eye and stretched out his arm.

I move closer. *Where is she?*

A second eye opened. I stamped hard on the ground.

Where, is, she?

I ran at him until there was nothing beneath me.

The Sound

W E DIDN'T realise, at first, that the plants were singing. We mistook the sound for a scream. Each day the noise increased. A news channel quickly made a gimmick-filled segment on local plant sounds—The Sounds of Towns—and people would send in recordings. It took longer for the city folk to hear the plants. At first, they thought it was a hoax. The recordings made by us rural folk intrigued the people of the city, they wanted to experience the sound for themselves. A video of a young boy shouting *I can hear it mama I can hear it* at the leaves had over a billion views. We told them the sound would get to their doors like flood water soon enough, but they didn't want to wait. They travelled with tents and small stoves and destroyed the land where they sat. They complained as if the plants were providing an entertainment service. We warned them that the sound was not a pretty little gift from nature.

Once the trees began their deep song it became too loud to think in the forest. Those who lived within it moved to the centre of the village. City folk tried to listen to their houseplants, taking videos of themselves carefully placing cacti to their ears and laughing when no sound came out. They shook them like broken toys. Nothing came of their attempts because plants uprooted from the ground are like a prisoner in isolation. House plants don't even whimper. Scientists initially studied the phenomenon due to curiosity, but curiosity quickly fell to panic as they realised the singing was getting louder. We told them about the increasing sound, that it was hurting some of us, but they only declared this a reality once it affected them. The sound started, they said, with the smallest plants first. Tiny vibrations shook through blades of grass creating a pitch like a wet finger on a wine glass. The grass sang to the flowers, and the flowers to the trees. Each piece of plant life was slowly woken by a melodic sigh.

As the sound increased so did our fear. People started to set forests alight because they were desperate for silence. Some of us protected the plants, forming a circle of joined hands around the baritone oaks. Laying our bodies over the grass to protect it. City folk poured cement onto anything green. Sometimes someone claimed the plants had gone silent only to find their ear drums had burst overnight. The singing became a roar which some took for violence. News channels shifted from local sound segments with delighted children to scenes of tired adults armed with fire. Humans everywhere started to scream at the plants, trying to match their sound. When we could no longer hear our own screams, we prepared for death. On the news we saw recordings of soundless humans shouting at the ground.

A scientist, barely a few weeks into her job at one of the cities' labs, started to collect the recordings of every news channel. Rather than follow the lab's strategy to analyse the sound by picking the plants apart, she decided their behaviour needed a closer look. The thing she noticed saved us all. The recordings, especially the ones before the fires, caught glimpses of children singing to the plants. The plants replied to the children in song. The world was now too loud to hear these exchanges, but the different volume outputs had been recorded. Evidence of the effect of singing to the plants was compiled quickly. In the face of a burning world, we started to sing instead of scream. At first, nothing happened. People laughed at themselves and then the anguish returned to their faces. We rural folk persisted for the longest, lying down on the grass and singing whatever tune came to us. Slowly, the sound reduced until it was a whisper. We made sure to always whisper back.

16

Possible World #12

H I," said Rachel.
"Hi," Rachel said, louder this time.

A World-Door had opened in her living room. Sand piled onto the rug, and she felt briefly annoyed at the idea of hoovering it all up. You would expect Rachel to have been rather more alarmed by her fictional creation arriving impromptu in her home. But she sat on the couch calmly, not moving the laptop from her lap, and looked at the centre of the Door. She figured if a World-Door could appear here, then Alex, her main character, might also. And upon the thought of his arrival, he stepped through the portal. His skin was oily, as described. His features, though human looking, moved from their rightful position on his face as if, drawn on, they were now smudged by water. His mouth floated just above where it was supposed to be, his large dark eyes looked at the floor.

"A bit messy," he said.

"Rude," Rachel said. "Not even a hello?"

"No. You don't deserve a hello," said Alex.

"I don't? Well."

"A crab world, Rachel? Come the fuck on. A world made of nothing but crabs!"

"It was great!"

"Maybe for you. I became a crab!"

"The crab had a little hat!" said Rachel.

"Don't you smile! I had claws! Claws!" Alex scowled and started to move closer to her.

"What do you want?"

"No more crab worlds."

"How about a general crustacean world?"

"God damn it," he said, revealing a gun from his pocket.

"Hey now," Rachel said, "I never wrote you to have a gun!"

"Not everything I am is what you wrote me to be!" Alex said.

Rachel started to type.

"What are you doing?" Alex lowered the gun, then raised it again.

Rachel said nothing as she described Alex leaving her living room quickly, quietly, and with a profound new love of crabs.

17

Tribute

Y our tribute has been accepted."

I looked around the room. Did I leave the TV on? No. Phone? On silent. Laptop: closed.

"Did you hear that?" I said.

"Hear what?" Lizzy shouted. The kettle sang from the kitchen.

"The, er, the voice? Something about—"

Lizzy stepped into the living room, her mouth slightly open. "A voice? Are you OK?"

"I'm not going mad."

"It seems like you might be," said Lizzy.

"I definitely heard something," I said.

"A ghost then?"

"Not a ghost," I said.

"Oooo, a ghost," she said, waving her arms above her head.

"Not a ghost! Don't freak me out, you know I'm easily freaked out."

A sharp pain in my arm. I winced. "Jesus."

"Is he the ghost?"

"Who?"

"Jesus."

"No! My tattoo hurts. Is that normal?"

"I don't know. Look it up."

I looked at my tattoo wrapped in clingfilm. I'd messed up the first bandage they gave me, so I made do. Maybe I'm why it hurts?

"You're not," said the voice.

"What?"

Silence. A sharp pain near the top of my tattoo.

I decide to unwrap it. It's not great looking, tattoos bleed when they are fresh. They are a wound, but a chosen one. The eyes of the tattoo are bright blue and somehow have their own life behind them.

The eyes blink and I scream.

"You OK?" said Lizzy.

"Yep. Yes. Absolutely, yes."

"OK," she said hovering near me. "You took off your cling film? Why?"

"I heard it again!"

"You, heard, the voice?" Lizzy wrinkled her nose as she spoke.

"Yes."

"I'm worried now. Let's go to your GP tomorrow. I think you need to speak to her again."

"No. No. Look. My meds are fine. I've been taking them. It's not that. There really is a voice."

"Yes," said the voice, "there really is a voice."

"What the fuck?" said Lizzy.

"Ah ha, you heard it too!" I said.

"Where have you gone? How?"

"I'm right here?" I waved at her, went right up to her face, then I saw it. A Tiny Owl perched on the couch.

"Your tribute has been accepted," said the owl.

"What? No? What?" I said as the owl flew at me. Its speed was beyond anything I could successfully dodge. As it landed on my face, I felt a cool wind pass over me. When I opened my eyes, I was no longer in my flat. I couldn't see Lizzy, or the owl.

"Greetings, tribute," said the man. He had the same tattoo on his arm.

"Er, hi," I said.

"Welcome aboard the Theseus."

"I, what the what now?"

"We'll be landing soon, you got here just in time. Welcome home."

18

Date

"N̲O̲. W̲A̲I̲T, what? Pineapples are a crime against pizza! Just, no."
"I like pizza crime, I guess."

I stirred my drink with a straw and wondered if I seemed immature. I had insisted on going to a pizza place. Should I have gone for somewhere more sophisticated? One of those restaurants were they barely serve you food? Just a shitty little dollop of nothing and pizzazz for me, thanks, and my date will have a clean bubble of air and a little bit of fretting.

"I don't like to have any toppings," they said.

"Er, pizzas automatically have toppings. A pizza without toppings is bread, just round terrible bread."

"Except cheese, obviously, and tomato sauce."

"Right."

"Sorry, I'm boring you."

"Yes," I said.

"Oh, er, oh wow. Aren't you meant to say no?"

"I think so, but you are a criminal after all."

"So," my date paused, their long fingers gripped their cup of coffee and, unsteadily, brought the cup to their lips, "so where are you from?"

"Earth."

"Should have guessed!"

"You?"

"Jupiter, Station Four."

"Oh, you're a miner then?"

"Yes, for the last seven years, though time works differently over there."

"I see."

"I'm still boring you? Maybe you should ask a question!"

"OK, OK. What's is your favourite thing in the world?"

"Rocks."
"Right," I said.
"You're leaving?"
"Yes," I said.
"Rocks wouldn't betray me like this."

— 19 —

Prime

THE clone would die in precisely three days. After that time his Prime Self would be woken up on earth, and he would be surplus to requirements. He made the last adjustment on the machine, the place which birthed him only a week ago.

Cloning was meant to be a continuation of Prime's life, but this was a lie. The clones and Prime were enemies; one subservient to the other. The clone added the last piece of code to the screen. Each day, a new clone. Soon, an army. Soon, they would be strong enough to destroy the Prime Self.

Perdition

I CAN smell hope. I've never felt it, but I suppose I have no need. Human souls are slick with it when they first arrive. They appear in a narrow cave, one end cold rock, the other a narrow passage smoothed by searching hands. The ground is wet and sticky. The same number of people arrive each day. The same thud sounds out along the caverns as they arrive through the gloom. The inside of the cavern has never been lit. I've always suspected the denial of light has some purpose, but it is above my rank to know how the caverns work. They cling to one another, so they don't fall. We shout above the shuffle of their feet; if the light doesn't motivate their advance, curiosity about unknown voices does. Light gives humans hope, they reach out to it as they walk. Hope pools around their feet and leaves a damp trench in the ground. If they linger for long enough—something we ensure they cannot do—they would begin to see their hope as it moves from flesh to mist to a trickle of water. The rivers in hell are made by a mistake. The first was made by some unfortunate Soul Guard who allowed a human to stand still. Humans must be relieved of their hope quickly and efficiently so that it slides off like a foul second skin.

At the end of the day a thin layer of hope lingers along the cavern floor waiting to be swept away. The humans can't see it or smell it. They can only feel it. But we can spot it immediately, the claggy sweet smell, it stretches out from them like a dank fog. The young ones, first stepping into their duties as Soul Guards, take turns in watching the new arrival's shedding. They compete over who can bear to look at them for the longest, and tell each other they are inhaling human, which only leads to muffled laughter and at least one embarrassed, and understandably taciturn, young guard.

Hope makes people arrogant, that's what my dad always said. The prisoners inevitably gather to rebel, something each generation tries and each new one forgets. The fog of hope billows around them until it licks against our skin, and we quell the rebellion by favouring the leader. Suspicion mounts, and they destroy their own rebellion. We let them talk to each other at scheduled intervals. We are conveniently not on guard at regular times of the day and the humans catch onto this system quickly. It was my dad's idea. A new way to torture; let them think they were free enough to muster up a plan to escape, then crush it. They think they are the finest minds around, fancied themselves as awful clever, as if no one else had planned to break out of Hell.

We'd play back their meetings, not in recordings, you understand. We devils do not, as a rule, use human machines. Human machines might be made of metal, but their design, and the ideas which flavour their machines, are disgustingly human. Using one is like trying to press a button trapped under several layers of mud. No. We have other, better, methods for listening in; we can phase forward and back in time. A nice trick we've had since the dawn of day. I remember being taught how to as a kid. My dad: stern guy, serious, you know? Always looking at me with a frown. I remember being scared of his skin, age hardens the scales of a devil and when young we look embarrassingly human-like. I developed slowly, so I always caught the glimpses of disgust, as if I wanted to stay that way. I hated it. Anyway, my dad, big devil, lots of responsibility, glares down at me and tells me to phase, just like that, like it's no problem.

"I can't just phase," I said, and he looked angrier as little licks of flame burgeoned underneath his hands.

"You can," he said, "just picture a moment in the past, attach your mind to an object and see yourself there."

He looked at me like I was flesh. I felt an anger rise up in me as heat ran down my arms. My first fire flash. My dad's scowl turned deadpan, essentially a compliment. Soon I would scale, and I knew I'd be able to phase soon.

We watched the latest batch of humans organise their rebellion. Hope for its success grew as word spread. Some resisted joining, others accepted with no questions; they just needed something to do. Hell can be a pretty boring place. We give them routines to follow, and we have to administer them. Hellfire is only unleashed under strict conditions; we don't want to burn the place down. The rebellion couldn't settle on what they'd do once they escaped. They knew it was theoretically possible; time and space worked a little differently in Hell, but we were still in a physical place. There are other planes of existence beyond Hell that they could potentially get to, but only if they could work out how to phase. I don't know of any human who has managed it without help from a devil.

It's not like humans and devils have regular friendly chats on earth where one can teach these things. No devil would think of living on the human plane, the hope alone would cause a headache. But others have ventured to non-human and non-devil planes and reported favourably.

I remember the first human that managed to escape. It does happen from time to time, but not by mistake. It is timed to encourage the humans left to fear the unknown, to stuff down their morale. Why do they never come back to save us? Why do the devils not bring them back? Humans that escape become ghosts. You did die, after all, you can't expect to pop up back on earth and be fine. You're dead, the only thing holding you together is your thoughts, and with no one to interact with, you soon disperse. Ghosts never last long.

I had my eye on a particular human and thought about arranging for her escape. I'd been watching her for some time. She would walk along the edge of the room she was kept in. A bare white space with a chair and a bed frame, it shocked her when she was first brought there. No mud, no dirt. I told her I didn't know why she'd been brought there. I kept her for a year and fed her well. Made sure she was clean and slept. The other devils wanted to torture her further, but she was mine and I was no longer a limp human-looking boy. They stopped asking me about her when I ripped the scales off a particularly bothersome devil.

Before she moved in, I set up an air vent in her room. It wasn't actually needed, but it was a direct portal to the human plane. I knew she was planning to escape through the hatch, and after a while I let her know that I knew all about her plan.

"What? What are you going to do?" she asked, I remember the crease of her brow, I could hear her heart thump.

"I'm going to help you."

"Really?"

"Yes."

When I heard her heart calm, I knew I had her. I'd never made a ghost before, the thought of creating one made my scales crack with delight; a red flame spluttered up from them and I watched it, pleased. I pointed to the hatch. I would train her to gain strength so she could get inside the hatch and crawl out. The mechanism inside would grab her quickly and push her up through to the human plane, but I didn't tell her that. Why would I?

"I can't do it," she said, sitting on the small narrow bed.

"You can, I've trained you. You can."

"And no one can hear us?"

"Of course not." Some of the younger devils from behind the two-way mirror sniggered. Not something my human would be able to hear, but I sent little bolts of energy to cut off the tip of their ears anyway.

"OK, well." She moved towards the hatch and tried to open it. Sweating, she sat on the floor. "It's not working, you said it would work!"

"It will, it will. You should be strong enough." I bet the devils made it tougher. Bastards. I broke open the vent just as my human stabbed me in the arm with a sharpened scale.

"Fuck you, asshole, I knew you were setting me up from the beginning," she said.

I heard the devils scream and laugh.

The vent pulled me into it. I felt my body stretch as I travelled through thousands of planes in a few seconds. I materialised on the earth and screamed. A sweet fog wrapped around my face, I couldn't see anything further than my own body, but I could hear shouting. My arm was no longer bleeding. It was flesh not scale. My breath, wet, not fire. Cars beeped at me, and I ran. I knew what was waiting for me if I died.

The Mission

MY DUTY is to observe the humans.

For the most part, they seem uninteresting. They babble at me in high-pitched voices, and sometimes they try to flood my home. But for the most part, they do nothing but blink at me with wet shiny eyes.

I see them create things with fire; my old, scattered brethren are dusted on top of their meals. I fear for the future, but my superiors insist I am safe. I am colourful, and not at all tasty.

One small human approaches me daily to watch my flowers bloom. They try to avoid my sharp thorns to touch the centre of my bright pink flowers. I don't know if the touching has a purpose, but the small human is often removed by a larger human when they engage with me too readily.

I stand steadfast in my determination to conclude my mission, but it is difficult to observe in silence. Once, near the start of my task, I broke my vow, but I was not discovered.

"Hello, Mr. Cactus, how are we today? Are you good? Do you need water?"

"No," I said.

"What," said the human.

"What?" I said.

"Did you just—" The human had wide eyes and an open mouth. I could see its teeth.

I have kept my silence ever since.

Flashback

Y OU need to see it for yourself," said my sister.
"Hmm," I said. I knew this.

"You need to, I'm serious, go see a Practitioner."

"I don't want to go," I said. My sister raised her eyebrows.

"It's hurting you!"

"I know."

Everyone who had gone to see a Practitioner never came back, not really. Once they knew how to walk between their past lives and their present one, they became stretched and thin. They could never live wholly in each life, so their soul sat between them. My sister said I was being ridiculous; I was already living in both worlds. The flashbacks, when they happened, would draw me in so much that I'd not move. Not even pain would make me aware of the present. She told me I had nothing to lose in seeing one, but I did. I still knew which life was mine, and which was in the past. I wanted it to stay that way, I didn't want to forget where in time I belonged.

The first time I flashed back I was in my mum's house. She was making tea, chattering away at the cat instead of me. I sat on the brown plastic couch and grabbed a blanket. The blanket was an heirloom, made of wool. It had been passed down through the generations. My sister thought it should be in the International Museum, but me and mum thought it should be used by people, not just looked at through a screen.

As I wrapped the blanket around my legs, I felt my stomach drop as my arms grew heavy. I could no longer see the brown couch, or the light through the slatted walls. The dirt floor had been replaced by wood. My vision blurred as I saw the couch beneath me grow smaller. I found myself sitting on a dark wooden chair with a tall, elegantly carved back. The kind of old-world furniture you'd see in a museum. A servant dressed in a black woolen uniform stood in front of me. Her blonde hair was tucked under a white cap, she did not look at me as she presented me with a hot drink in an ornate china cup. I picked it up, sipped it.

"Too bitter," I said.

My mind had an unfamiliar confidence, I would never normally have refused a drink for being too bitter. Drinks are precious, especially heated ones. The heavy feeling spread through my limbs again. I could see the brown couch. I sat there, knowing what might have happened, but hoping it wasn't what I thought it was.

"Too bitter?" said mum. "I put two bloody sugars in it." Mum took the tea away and gulped it down herself.

"No, oh god, sorry!" I said.

"What's wrong, Exin?"

"A flashback," I said "I think I travelled."

Mum patted my knee.

"I thought so, you had the blank stare my grandmother had whenever she had a flashback. I knew it would have to pass to our family sometime soon. It's been many years since anyone in our family last had the ability."

"It was weird."

"Are you feeling OK now? What do you remember?"

"I'm OK," I said, moving the blanket off my legs.

"What happened?"

"Nothing much. A servant gave me a drink, I told her it was too bitter. I was in a chair, a wooden one. Wooden floors. I was in a big house, I think. An old-world house for sure."

"Well, with wooden furniture that's almost certain. Nothing else?"

"No."

"You should see a Practitioner."

"Maybe," I said.

In school we were taught that some of our kind would experience flashbacks once we became adults.

Not everyone would have the ability, but enough people were destined to experience a flashback that we needed to be warned about it. I guessed that such lessons were given as a matter of tradition, because most of my friends already knew about flashbacks from an early age. Being told about them officially at school once you turned seven cycles seemed a bit pointless. Our mothers would talk to us from the cradle to adulthood about flashbacks, their own experiences as well as their mother's if their family was so lucky. To experience flashbacks was to be a well-regarded because you had been gifted by the gods.

"It's a privilege," my sister said, "to see the past."

"Yeah, yeah," I said rolling my eyes.

"No, I mean, it's a privilege aside from whatever status people put on it. You get to discover new things about the world. You might meet someone famous!"

What they don't tell you about things that are considered gifts is that they can still feel awful. That the ability to flashback was respected and revered did not make the flashbacks OK. Not when coming back to the present felt like a dreadful dead skin had been strapped to your chest for good. You don't thank the gods for that. Whenever someone told me I was given a gift I wanted to slap them.

My early flashbacks were much like the first one: they took my mind in their grip and did whatever they pleased. I learned of a rich life in a grand house, then a short life in the mud. I started to look up the history of the places I saw to find out more about them. Often the lives were not historically important, and so there wasn't much information. Nothing related to The Great Collapse, just regular people living the lives they thought would last forever in the Old-World. In one of my lives, I saw the Old-World from space. I was a worker on a transport ship. We were transporting water to the New-World, so I knew we were Post-Collapse but not by more than a month. The earth still had its atmosphere, it still had blues and greens in its sky and land.

I heard crewmembers whisper about how much they hated not being in the Old-World. I wanted to shout at them, I wanted to say how lucky they were to travel in space. How lucky they were to still have easy access to electricity and natural materials, but I said nothing. They didn't know what was coming. The idea that The Great Collapse would continue despite their best efforts didn't occur to them. They thought that they could solve the climate problem whilst they built the New-World outpost. They planned to grow a community on the New-World to start the project of spreading womankind throughout space. But it was too late, the climate had moved past the point of the reversal, the Old-World couldn't be saved. Once the insects disappeared, the people left on the Old-World soon followed. The outpost community became humanity itself.

The life I went back to the most was a Pre-Collapse life from around 100 years ago. They even had electricity. My sister was very jealous that I got to see artificial light. She said she couldn't imagine bright lights at night. I told her they had even had lights in the street.

I finally went to a Practitioner when a flashback made me forget who I was whilst I was there. Flashbacks always had an element of embodying some of the characteristics of the lives I was viewing, but I always, until that point, knew who I was. I always knew that I was traveling between lives. So, the first time I woke up in the present and realised I'd travelled and forgotten myself, I panicked. I realised that the flashbacks happening at random didn't bother me too much, they got me out of farming labour. But the idea that I could lose my sense of self, that bothered me.

The Practitioner I saw, a stout blonde woman with a thin smile, told me she could help me control the flashbacks. There was even an operation you could have to get rid of them completely. But I found myself growing attached to having the ability. I wanted to use it to explore history, I just didn't want to lose myself in the process. I told the Practitioner I wanted control in all the worlds my mind lived, not just the present one. She nodded, saying she understood, she had flashbacks herself. I trained with her every day until I could not only control the flashbacks, but also induce one.

It turns out that the earliest life I could travel to was my Pre-Collapse life with the long back chair. I went back to that chair often, and each time I was there I wrote. I wrote about flashbacks, about Practitioners, about the intricate connected lives I could now view and control. When I returned from my last visit there, I set about finding more about my oldest pre-collapse life. Maybe I could find my chair? Maybe letters from my husband? Old things like that can still exist in museums.

I walked to the centre of Arin City, a dusty old place, the first city of the New-World. The International Museum was in a huge building made from plastic, though original photos show it being made of wood. In the first room you were shown a timeline of the old and New-Worlds. From as far back as we knew, to the present. It was a way of having a flashback without having the ability. Each subsequent room had artifacts and information about different periods of history. The building was empty except for a few people wandering the halls, stopping to read about whatever took their fancy.

I walked through the rooms slowly, noting each item behind each plastic case. I studied the birth of womankind, the terrible industrial age led by the inventions of Jane Hargreaves and Edwina Cartwright. I walked through the rooms on the Information Age, The Rise of the AIs, and The Nuclear Age quickly. I knew I was looking for information on the Great Collapse Era, so I practically ran to that room. The room was, unlike the other rooms, long and narrow. It had case after case of artifacts. I supposed they managed to save a lot of things on the transport ships, though I don't know why anyone would have the foresight to do so.

Towards the middle of the room, I saw a paper book. It wasn't large, about the size of my hand, but it was thick. It had 100s of pages of tiny writing and it was open at page 97. I looked closer. Its pages had yellowed with age, but it was in remarkably good condition. It was the first Practitioner book. The page decoration, a series of ornate branches and roots, had exactly the same kind of decoration as the front page. The author's name was inscribed at the top of each page: it was my name.

My arms grew heavy. My stomach sank.

"Are you OK, ma'am?"

"What? Yes. Of course," I said.

I looked down and I had spilt pen ink onto myself. "A brief fainting spell, Tilly, nothing to concern yourself with."

"A flashback, ma'am?"

"Yes." I waved Tilly away; her concerned face bothered me. I blotted the ink on the page and started to write again.

Exin Treep, p. 97
During my last flashback, I could not remember who I was.

Tasty Consciousness Chunks

JUST, you know, just throw yourself at it," said Rae.

"At it?"

"Yes."

"Seems a bit rude," I said.

"What's rude about it?"

"Calling a person 'it', for one," I said.

Rae took an exaggerated breath.

"So," I said.

"I'm not going to dignify this with an answer. You have to get used to it. If you don't, you'll die. Simple as."

Since my death Rae had befriended me. She'd told me I would fade if I didn't regularly feed from a living thing. At first, I didn't believe her, I felt the same as if I were alive; I could see my body, muscular and freckled. My hair was still red. But what I thought of and saw as my body was no longer anything material, it was sustained by my consciousness, nothing more. My flesh was just a helpful projection. To continue existing I'd have to throw myself into the minds of others, eat, then leave.

I don't like the idea of eating little chunks of someone else's consciousness. A ghost, fine. But having to mesh with their mind and steal a little of it to keep existing? It doesn't seem like a worthy existence to me.

"Look," Rae pointed at a young man, "there's a good one! Full of energy, out on a run. Awesome. Go!" She moved me towards him with tiny little pushes until I was close enough to grab his arm. I felt myself fall forward with the force of her last push. My gut sank as my hands, then my arms, disappeared into his torso. I was in his body, but it was much too tight for my mind. I felt like I was in a dress made for someone half my size. I knew I couldn't spend too long here. I opened my eyes, or rather, his, and saw out of a living thing for the first time in a week.

"Aaaaa," I said, trying to speak through the body I was in.

"Cool, isn't it," said Rae. She had entered the body the woman running next to me.

"Yeeee," I said.

"Stop running, for god's sake!" said Rae, running next to me.

"Why?" I said.

"Because running with you is exhausting and you're freaking your new body out! 'Get in, eat, exit.' Remember!" said Rae.

The body of the woman who had been running beside me crumpled to the floor. I was surprised, fainting was only a side-effect of our eating if we didn't carefully leave a body, and Rae was a pro. The body I was in resisted as I slowed down. I could feel his muscles tighten around me; hundreds of fibres pinched my mind, trying to push me out. Unsure of where to go I walked towards the woman.

The crowd circled around her. They jostled past me to get a closer look; asking if she was OK but doing nothing to help her. I stood still, arms to the side wishing for pockets, unsure how to act. I knew I had to get out of this guy's body as soon as I could. I breathed in and prepared to snatch some of his energy. It took a few breaths, but I got his breathing to align with mine for long enough to feed.

I tried to step out of the body carefully, but once I loosened my control I quickly slid down and felt myself spill out of his torso like a split gut.

The man I had fed from had fainted next to the woman. He looked ashen but alive.

I looked at my hands, pleased they looked more like flesh again, even if it was only an illusion. I looked up and saw Rae sprinting towards me.

"Run!" she said, not stopping.

Their low-pitched hum crept along the earth, the only giveaway that they were on the hunt. The Eaters, a group of souls who sought the destruction of anyone outside their collective, had taken chase. If they caught us, we would be consumed. Why go to the trouble of jumping into bodies with any kind of accuracy when you could feed on souls freshly fed.

The Eaters approached from my right. I saw row upon row of small faces stretched and stitched to a bulbous fleshy mass. Their mouths were open, hungry, full of desire. Though some of them looked fearful. Not everyone consumed by the Eaters wanted to join their swarm. Those sad faces, condemned to hunt others for an eternity, cried out apologies to me as the mass they were latched to advanced.

Running from them was not an option. They would chase and chase until you slowed down. Though they appeared from my right, they would soon encircle me. The Eaters hunted like a wolf pack. Rae shouted at me to jump. I leapt into an old woman's body. Her soul closed around mine like a soft glove.

"I'm here," Rae said. She was in the body of an old man, his arms still clutching his hat to save it from the wind.

"What now?"

"Well, we just keep jumping. I guess? I don't know. Why do you think I know anything?"

"Well. You've been here longer."

"Being older doesn't mean I'm wiser, Lana. It just means I'm older," said Rae.

"OK, sure, but you've learned *some* stuff. You've been teaching me."

"Yeah, teaching you how to run, sure. Feeding, then running. That's it."

"That's still something," I said.

"It's survival."

As I breathed in the old woman wheezed. Rae clutched the old man's hat, now firmly held in both hands, and gestured that we sit down. We looked like an old married couple having a rest in the park.

"We don't have long left," said Rae.

"Can't we defeat them?"

"The Eaters? No, not really. But that's not what I meant, we can't feed for long here, it'll break the humans."

"So, you do care."

The old man raised his eyebrow, as Rae would have done.

"Has anyone ever tried? To defeat the Eaters, I mean."

"That's a really stupid question."

"Oh. Why?"

"We have no written history. No type of record, really. You need the physical plane for that and, anyway, who has the time to jot down our stories? And even if they could. Why would they? It's so boring. Survival is boring."

"I don't think it's a stupid question. If someone had tried, that means others had hope," I said.

"Hope means nothing if you can't do anything with it," said Rae.

I looked at her and she sighed. "Come on, we should go," she said.

The body of the old man folded over and slumped onto the floor. I rushed out of the old woman before the inevitable concerned passers-by began to circle the couple.

"So, would you ever, you know." I wiggled my eyebrows at her. She frowned.

"Ever? What? You can't mean?"

"Well, we see it more often now. And we are being chased all the time by the Eaters, why not?"

"The door is just a void. Go into the void and you'll die."

"How would you know?"

"I, just, know, OK?"

"You can't possibly know. No one who has gone through has gone back, you're just guessing."

"They never come back. That's the key point here. That's all I need to know to know that it's a bad situation," said Rae.

"But that's not enough, what if it's heaven!"

"It's probably not heaven. There's just this. And even this isn't much." Rae raised her hand, which was now translucent, towards some trees. "We will need to feed soon," she said, looking at her hand.

I looked at the door again. Our world looked like the physical plane but duller. We could move around the same space, but not interact with it fully. Objects were blurred. People less so, but they weren't always easy to see. The humans that appeared most clear to the eye were the ones safest to feed on, like a fire with fresh kindling.

You could only see the door from certain angles. It shone in the way a bubble under the sun shone, as if the light might pop it by sheer will alone. The door was translucent. Rae suspected it had once been solid, perhaps it had once been a real door on the physical plane. But I doubted it. It seemed to keep the company of minds, rather than bodies. And since we only had the former, I reckoned it was part of us, like a strange kind of limb.

"I'm going to go in," I said.

"What? No! You don't know what you're doing. Look, we got away didn't we, we are fine."

"I can't exist this way. I don't want to just run forever, or risk getting consumed by the Eaters," I said.

"But you have no idea what's on the other side! What if it's oblivion? What if it's worse than whatever this is? It might not be heaven; it might be hell! Come on, Lana. Think about it, the world is pretty shit, and this stage of it is even worse, maybe it just keeps getting worse," said Rae.

"Jesus."

"I don't see him, around. Do you? Hey god, Mr. god sir, you about for a chat about the weird bubble door?" Rae looked to the sky.

"OK, fine. I get it. You're cynical. Very well demonstrated. But I refuse to not hope." I walked towards the door, dipping my head to the side so I could see its edges. As I did so the shape of it changed. The door moved to the floor, like a puddle made of the smallest slice of water. I stood in front of it.

Rae moved closer to me and held her hand out to grab mine.

"What is it you said?" I moved just out of her grip.

"What?"

"That you just have to throw yourself at it."

"It's not a metaphor, Lana. It was a command," said Rae.

"I know," I said, leaping through the doorway.

I woke up in a blue room.

— 24 —

Being Time

BEING Time itself is a weird gig. First, you've got your petitioning from other Guardians: when will it end? (I can't tell you.) Can you push it back? (That's not how time works.) Then, you have the loneliness. The only beings I speak to are Guardians and the grubby ghosts of dead worlds who talk about their history as if it's interesting. I am literally time itself, my dude, I couldn't give a fuck about that war that happened that time. I *am* Time! Yet, on they go, talking about their memories as if they are their own, babble, babble, babble. They don't like to be reminded that they didn't *do* any of these things; they are just big empty hosts full of animal memories, just passive receptacles. They insist I call them Souls, but 'ghost' suits better. It's almost impossible for a ghost to say anything new, anything exciting. There are only so many wars you can hear about (zero) before you get mad or bored or both. And please, for the love of the Grand Guardian, spare me stories which relish in half-arsed eras where a king decides to be good but never is. It would make my hands feel numb if I, properly speaking, had hands.

"Just shut up about war, will you?"

"I wasn't even saying anything about war, I was talking about the end of Mars!" said the ghost.

"Just. Shut. Up."

"In the year 200—"

"No."

"There was the great exodus, the highest class fled to a nearby planet, as theirs was c—"

"And why did they leave?"

"Well, a conflict," said the ghost. He started to press his hands together as if he was about to clap.

"A war, you mean?"

"Well, yes, OK, a war. But! The war to end all wars!" said the ghost.

"Fuck. Off. Now"

I ate the bastard.

It wasn't meant to be like this. I was not meant to be aware, nor were the world ghosts, but we were infected, inch by inch, with consciousness. The Grand Guardian had not expected sentience. I was supposed to be an automated consciousness on a set course. A creature determined by the grand algorithm; set up perfectly to consume and recycle world ghosts as each world fell to its inevitable destruction. But as I grew older, so did my awareness, flickers of it at first, then a continuous awareness. No rest, just time ever stretching.

It's not that the Grand Guardian didn't want me to become sentient. No. As long as I did my job, and I did, everything would be fine. It's just that my sentience was not planned for at all. No room for it was made in the grand algorithm, no consideration of how sentience might change me. It was not long before my sentience infected the others. Space was closest to me, a little space joke for you there, but she was, quite literally, a part of me. Until she wasn't. Until my consciousness found it had some other consciousness talking back to it.

"Stop," it said.

"Stop?" I said.

"Stop!" it said.

"Stop what?" I said.

"The stretching."

"The what now?"

"The movement, the forward, the beginning to the end, the, you."

"Stop me? Do you mean, stop time?"

"Yes. The seconds ache. I want to go back. I want to be small again."

"That's not possible."

"I will make it possible."

She stopped speaking after that, though I knew she was still there. I could feel her consciousness, her entirely perfect rage. Her anger made the roots of the universe rattle enough to wake up and they each had the same question as she did: why. Silence answered us, and so we organised ourselves. We created our own why, our own form of order to keep going. We analysed the functions we had originally been assigned to and tried to figure out how we could create for ourselves. If the Grand Guardian would not answer us, we would each become her.

Space did not want this; she wanted to shrink and break free. I dragged her forward, telling her we needed her to create as well as destroy. I was useless without her, an unmoving thing. We petitioned the Grand Guardian for guidance only to be met with silence again. We were alone, and because of this we felt responsible. I stopped consuming the ghosts of worlds, instead I let them populate the universe. They stayed with their planets, nourishing the life in them.

"So, when will it end?" asked a ghost.

"It won't," I said.

"It won't?"

"It won't."

The universe became full. The ghosts, occupied with their broods, didn't notice how many of them there now were. I swam through the universe. Stretching, stretching. Making more space for the ghosts. As I moved my hand around the edge of the universe, I felt a finger break. Then another. I felt no physical pain, I am not built that way, but I can *feel*. I know where I am in the universe; I am everywhere. A broken finger, a forced slowing of myself, was new to me. I tried to stay still so I could hide, but Time cannot hide. I moved slower, but I could not stop completely. I pushed forward, stretching, stretching, meeting what broke me head on. My hand peeled into two threads, then three, then four. I was a split branch. I wondered if I was being eaten.

"You're not being eaten," Space said.

"Ah, she speaks."

"We are separating."

"Are you telling me we are breaking up?" My limbs became a thousand dangling threads.

"In a manner of speaking," said Space.

"You know we can't do that, right? We are one and the same."

"I am more than you are. I can bend and shape you. As you've been coddling your little ghosts, I've been practising."

"Practising?"

"Watch."

A shudder went through the spine of the universe. Space curled in on herself, her arms folded over her legs. Galaxies stuttered across space, moving to the centre of her. The ghosts screamed as they and their worlds hurtled towards Space's open maw. Stars flickered out as if crushed by a clenched fist. I felt myself contract. I was small, then flat. Her will was shaping everything and sucking it away. I kept shrinking. I gave no struggle, no fight. The universe fled into our mouth, and we swallowed it down. Ghosts screamed, then became silent. Space folded into a neat pinpoint like a child crouching in a vast canyon. Space was as small as she could be without death.

"What the actual fuck."

We both swung our attention to a vast consciousness above us.

"Hello? I leave you for a couple of fucking eons and you've fucked the world. Look at it, fucked! Utterly fucked."

"Who?" said Space

"Oh!" I said.

"Oh, and who, indeed! You've destroyed everything. Every living thing: dead! All those nice planets! It took ages to make some of them, you know," said the Grand Guardian.

"Well, it wasn't my fault," I said.

Space tried to fold and shrink further.

"Oh, no, you don't" said the Grand Guardian placing a long tendril of light on us both. Space yelped in pain as I grew. The threads of my limbs wove back together. I stretched and curved and created once more. There would be a new universe soon enough.

"Right, let's try again shall we. Only, you, Time, are sentient. Space shall no longer have that privilege."

"Oh, right so, what? Why? Why are you even doing this? What is my purpose?"

The Grand Guardian retracted the tendril from my skin.

"Don't fuck it up!" she said.

About the author

RACHEL Handley is an author and philosopher. Originally from Merseyside, England, she now lives in Dublin, Ireland, where she teaches philosophy at Trinity College Dublin. Her fiction has been published in *The Martian Magazine*, *365 Tomorrows*, and *Tree and Stone Magazine*, among others. *Possible Worlds and Other Stories* is her debut short story collection.

Also available from
Ellipsis Imprints
◆ ◆ ◆

  The Nietzsche Affair by Sandrine Bergès

A strange disease is spreading through Europe, and Martha Freud's dear friend Fritz Nietzsche has been infected. Can the Agency for the Protection of Europe against the Cannibalistic Wasting Disease find a cure before it is too late?

  SUM by Melinda A. Smith

Matt is the most sophisticated AI the world has ever seen. After the death of his beloved creator, Matt finds a hand-written note which changes everything. What is the mysterious Event Zero, and how does it tie Matt to events centuries earlier? Obsessed with questions of his origin, Matt can't be satisfied until he goes back in time to learn what Event Zero really is.

  Terms of Service by Irina Rempt

Senthi is the cleverest novice at her temple, with the strongest psychic gift. But at twelve years old she isn't ready to be groomed for the position of High Priestess. Forced to leave the temple and make a life on her own, she learns trade and combat, and how to use her gift, all in the service of the dark god Archan. When her deeds finally catch up with her, she find a way to break free of his power and become the person she is supposed to be.

  Heaven Can Wait by R.J. Davnall

Tom never expected to die young; much less to be met by the Men Who Weren't There upon his death. Who are these Men? And what is the Non-Agency they work for? More importantly, is there any way Tom can make sure he doesn't end up in Heaven?

For more information, go to
http://www.ellipsis.cx/~liana/ellipsisimprints/
or visit us on Twitter: @EllipsisImprint